WAYNE STINNETT

LOOTED

A JESSE MCDERMITT NOVEL

CARIBBEAN ADVENTURE SERIES, VOLUME 30

Copyright © 2025

Published by DOWN ISLAND PRESS, LLC, 2025

Beaufort, SC

Copyright © 2025 by Wayne Stinnett

All rights reserved. No part of this book may be reproduced, scanned, or distributed in any printed or electronic form without express, written permission. Please do not participate in or encourage piracy of copyrighted materials in violation of the author's rights. Purchase only authorized editions.

Library of Congress cataloging-in-publication Data

Stinnett, Wayne

Looted/Wayne Stinnett

p. cm. - (A Jesse McDermitt Novel)

ISBN: 978-1-956026-91-7

Cover, graphics, and interior design by Aurora Publicity

Edited by Marsha Zinberg, The Write Touch

Final Proofreading by Donna Rich

Published by Down Island Press, LLC

This is a work of fiction. Names, characters, and incidents are either the product of the author's imagination or are used fictitiously. Any resemblance to actual persons, living or dead, businesses, companies, events, or locales is entirely coincidental. Many real people are used fictitiously in this work, with their permission. Most of the locations herein are also fictional or are used fictitiously. However, the author takes great pains to depict the location and description of the many well-known islands, locales, beaches, reefs, bars, and restaurants throughout the Florida Keys and the Caribbean to the best of his ability.

If you'd like to receive my newsletter, please sign up on my website.
WWW.WAYNESTINNETT.COM.
Once or twice a month, I'll bring you insights into my private life and writing habits, with updates on what I'm working on, special deals I hear about, and new books by other authors that I'm reading.

.

THE GASPAR'S REVENGE
SHIP'S STORE IS OPEN 24/7.
There, you can purchase all kinds of swag
related to my books, and even my books themselves,
in whatever format you choose.
You can find it at
WWW.GASPARS-REVENGE.COM

Dedicated to Hoyt Platts.

It's said that cousins are a kid's first friends, but we never had the chance to develop a friendship until decades later. As the son of my mom's only brother, we never got to know one another until almost too late. I would give anything to have known you when we were boys.
Welcome to the family, cuz!

"My father used to play with my brother and me in the yard.
Mother would come out and say, 'You're tearing up the grass.'
'We're not raising grass,' Dad would reply. 'We're raising boys.'"
—Harmon Killebrew

ALSO BY WAYNE STINNETT

The Jerry Snyder Caribbean Mystery Series

Wayward Sons   Vodou Child   Friends of the Devil

The Charity Styles Caribbean Thriller Series

Merciless Charity	Enduring Charity	Elusive Charity
Ruthless Charity	Vigilant Charity	Liable Charity
Reckless Charity	Lost Charity	

The Jesse McDermitt Tropical Adventure Series16

A Seller's Market   Bad Blood   Cocaine Cowboys

The Jesse McDermitt Caribbean Adventure Series

Fallen Out	Rising Storm	All Ahead Full
Fallen Palm	Rising Fury	Man Overboard
Fallen Hunter	Rising Force	Cast Off
Fallen Pride	Rising Charity	Fish On!
Fallen Mangrove	Rising Water	Weigh Anchor
Fallen King	Rising Spirit	Swift and Silent
Fallen Honor	Rising Thunder	Apalach Affair
Fallen Tide	Rising Warrior	Dominica Blue
Fallen Angel	Rising Moon	Down Island
Fallen Hero	Rising Tide	Looted
	Steady as She Goes	

Rainbow of Collars Motivational Non-fiction Series

Blue Collar to No Collar   No Collar to Tank Top

The Florida Keys

Jesse's island in the Content Keys

CHAPTER ONE

November 24
South Side, Milwaukee, Wisconsin

The wind was frigid and right in his face as Will trudged along a seedy sidewalk in the less attractive part of town. His hoodie was over his head and his shoulders hunched forward, hands in his coat pockets.

As he walked, he passed the many boarded-up shops and warehouses that harkened to the city's industrial boom early in the previous century.

Most of the industry had long since moved overseas, and the shops that supported it had turned into a Walmart, then into malls out on the edge of town. Now, even the malls struggled, since people found it easier to do their shopping online.

It'd snowed heavily the previous night, almost eight inches. Then, during the day, the temperature had risen just enough above freezing to melt some of the snow into a slushy liquid, too thick to flow to the drains. The wet snow turned gray, thanks to the splatter of cars passing on the street, and had soaked through the sides of Will's sneakers and into his socks, causing a squishy sound with each step.

"I gotta find a way to get out of here," Will mumbled, stepping off the curb to cross the street. "Anywhere down south. This is my last damned winter here."

He'd made that promise to himself more than once, and here he was, just days before Thanksgiving, and he was still stuck in Milwaukee.

After passing another boarded-up and gated warehouse, half a block later, he turned into a dingy alley next to Lou's Tavern. Sheltered from the sun, the snow in the alley hadn't melted and crunched under his wet shoes.

Will banged on the first door he came to, steam billowing from his mouth and nostrils with each exhalation. He clutched his arms across his chest, rubbing them as he shifted his weight from one foot to the other.

Then he banged on the door again.

A narrow shaft of light spilled out into the snow-covered alleyway as someone inside moved the peephole cover and looked out.

"It's Will!" he shouted at the door, knowing whoever it was probably couldn't see him in the dark alley. "Open up, man! It's freezin' out here."

There was a clank as the steel bar bracing the closed door on the inside was lifted and placed on the floor. Then the door opened, spilling bright light into the alley and up the far wall.

Will stepped quickly into the bar's stockroom, stomping the slush from his sneakers on the weatherproof mat just inside the door.

"Another fuckin' winter in this hellhole," Kevin said, closing the door, then putting the bar back in place. "How'd we ever end up here in the first place?"

"What do you mean?" Will asked. "We grew up here."

"But why *here?*" Kevin persisted. "What the hell drew our grandparents to come to Milwaukee, of all places?"

It was a long, convoluted story, and Kevin had heard it from their parents as often as Will had.

Their father, Karl, had been born in Germany, but his brother Lucas was born in America. Will and Kevin's grandparents had immigrated to Wisconsin in the late 1960s, bringing little more than their first-born son with them. Granddad had carried the stigma associated with *his* father long enough.

Will and Kevin never knew their great-granddad. He'd been an officer in the German navy during World War II, and though he'd been conscripted and reportedly died in the line of duty, his young wife and their two children had been persecuted after the war.

Will's father had always dreamed of finding the place where his grandfather had died, convinced that the records were wrong, that he'd escaped Germany to bring his family to a place they could start over.

A few years ago, with the help of some computer nerd, their dad thought he had it all figured out and took off for Cuba, for Pete's sake, along with his brother and cousin, leaving the family high and dry for six months.

Will had been twenty-three at the time, Kevin was twenty-one, and their little sister, Lena, had been a senior in high school.

Karl and Lucas Crittenden had never returned from that trip to Cuba, and it was rumored that they'd spent several months there before going to the Gulf Coast of Florida. After that, the two brothers and their two cousins were never heard from again.

"Did Lou open the bar yet?" Will asked his brother, as he peeled off his coat.

"Doesn't seem much point," Kevin replied. "Only four people

have even walked past and they were hunched over and moving fast."

Will hung his coat up on a hook by the stockroom's heavy steel door. The stockroom was small, with the back wall stacked with cases of beer on the shelves of a metal rack, and the inside wall held cases of liquor, mostly brandy and whiskey.

Lou's Tavern was a simple bar, for simple, working-class people, and nobody ever ordered fruity cocktails with more than a couple of ingredients. It was a beer, brandy, or whiskey kind of place.

They had a jukebox that still played vinyl records, two pool tables, and an antique shuffleboard bowling machine that was older than Lou himself.

The door to the bar in the front swung open and Lou strode into the stockroom. "Good, you're here."

"Bitch of a cold night," Will said. "Kev was just sayin' it's slow."

"Like a Wisconsin winter, eh?" Lou grumbled. "Look, one of us three is gonna hafta go home, and I don't get paid a hourly wage, so me leavin' don't save me nothin'."

Kevin shrugged. "I'll go," he said to Will. "You took one last week."

"Not that it matters," Will said, removing his black apron from a hook and putting it over his head. "It takes both our wages for that crummy apartment."

"Thanks, kid," Lou said to Kevin. "My best to your sis." Then he turned to Will. "When ya get the door bolted, bring out a case of Miller Lite and two bottles of Korbel, eh?"

"Breaking out the good stuff?" Will asked, opening the door for Kevin. "I'll see you tonight, little brother."

"If we're just gonna sit here and drink and watch football," Lou replied, "then we might as well make the best of it."

As Lou turned and headed toward the door to the bar, Will called after him. "Who's playing?"

"Carolina at the Niners," he replied, pushing through the swinging door. "Bor-ring."

At the Miller rack, Will grabbed a case and placed it on the work bench, then selected two bottles of Korbel brandy, which wasn't the *best* in the world, but it wasn't cheap either. He placed the bottles on top of the four six-packs so they wouldn't roll, and as he was about to pick up the case, his phone rang.

Taking it out of his pocket, Will saw that the number display was just blank. Probably the old brick building blocking the signal.

He pressed *Accept* and held the phone to his ear anyway. "Hello?"

"You don't know me," a man's voice said with a strong "call center" type of accent.

Will was about to end the call when the man added, "I knew your father and uncle, Karl and Lucas."

"Who is this?" Will asked.

"My name is Manish Gupta," he replied. "And I can make you rich beyond your dreams."

"Yeah, right," Will retorted. "Look, I'm kinda busy right now. At work. A *real* job."

"Did you know that in 1945 your great-grandfather disappeared with a large quantity of pure gold?"

Will looked at the screen again. Still blank.

There'd been stories and rumors about his and Kevin's great-granddad. Outlandish gossip from the "old country" about great riches stolen from right under Hitler's nose.

Will's father had certainly believed the stories.

"Where'd you hear that?" Will asked, keeping his voice low.

Will's father had told him about how his great-granddad had

ended up the captain of a doomed submarine that disappeared in the North Sea. But Dad had always doubted that part of the story.

"It was what your father and uncle were trying to recover," the man on the phone said. "When they were both *murdered*."

"Murdered?" Will spat, then lowered his voice again. "My great-grandfather was lost at sea with his crew. What makes you think my *father* was murdered over it?"

"Because I was helping him and your uncle to find the gold," Gupta said, "but someone else got to them first."

"Oh yeah?" Will said.

"The gold's still out there," the mysterious voice replied. "Nobody has recovered it yet."

"Where did this happen?"

There was a short pause. "In the Everglades of Florida," Gupta finally replied. "I'll call again next week. Perhaps we can meet in person to talk about this."

The call ended and Will's phone returned to its usual lock screen.

"The *Everglades*," he whispered softly. "What the hell did you get into, Dad?"

CHAPTER TWO

Monday, December 1
Everglades National Park

An early morning mist hung over the dark, tannin-rich water, with just a few wispy tips of sawgrass visible above it, unmoving, as if trapped in a snowbank.

In the distance, a stand of bald cypress seemed to float on a snowy white cloud, the dozens of cypress knees that I knew would be around it, hidden in the fog.

The sawgrass usually waved and undulated with the lightest breeze, but there hadn't been a breath of it when I'd arrived the previous afternoon, and today didn't look all that promising either.

It was chilly, but not cold; about what you'd expect for this time of year in South Florida. The air aloft had been cooler, though. So I was wearing jeans and deck shoes in anticipation of getting back up into the clear blue sky.

From where I stood on *Island Hopper's* port float, I could see over the mist in all directions, and the morning sky was cloudless and beckoning. A perfect, dry December day for flying.

Taking off in a de Havilland Beaver float plane in the middle of the Everglades would necessitate being able to see the *water* as well as the sky, though. A floating log or dozing gator could make for a bad start to the day.

I watched as a bald eagle took flight from the high branches of the cypress stand, heading off to the north in search of breakfast. I envied his ability to soar above the fog, but he'd likely have a problem seeing anything in the water through it.

Although this day had been all planned weeks ago and dreamed of for two years, it was finally happening, and I couldn't quite believe what I was witnessing.

The natural beauty of the Everglades was marred by the hulking remains of a World War II-era German U-boat, its conning tower rising above the mist.

The submarine had lain on the bottom, buried in more than ten feet of mud, for eighty-one years, until Billy Rainwater came across it. Since then, he and Rusty, and occasionally myself and others, had been working on it, replacing wiring, batteries, motors, pumps, and seals, until we were finally able to blow the ballast tanks and raise her to the surface.

Savannah, Alberto, and I had spent last night aboard the sub, along with Rusty and Sid, our friends Billy and Trish, as well as a tugboat crew, and the ship's engineer, Herman Gottlieb.

Herman could read and understand some German, being of German descent, which had been invaluable during the restoration, since all the controls were labeled in German. He was from Mueller Township, a small community in Michigan's Upper Peninsula just north of Port Inland. He'd been born in the U.P., as had his parents, but his grandparents had immigrated there after the war.

The accommodation was far from ideal, but every corner of the sub, from the conning tower to the bilges, had been thoroughly scrubbed, dried, primed, and painted.

The old leather straps on the bunks had been replaced, along with an adequate number of mattresses, all with brand new bedding, so it was moderately comfortable. And by that I mean for a typical submariner who was much shorter than I was.

Knowing we'd be working late, we'd slept together in one of the tight crew compartments, one person per bunk. It was a little similar to what Rusty, Billy, and I had encountered on a naval warship during our South Pac cruise, when we'd all been stationed together in Okinawa, Japan. In short, it was cramped and claustrophobic.

But we'd made the best of it, talking late into the night, discussing plans and telling stories of other great finds.

But this one truly beat them all. An *intact*, diesel/electric German submarine, right here in South Florida. It'd remained hidden all that time, due to higher waters in the Glades, but two years ago, levels had reached about the lowest Billy had ever seen, exposing the top couple of feet of the conning tower.

The historical aspect of sleeping aboard an eighty-year-old German submarine wasn't lost to any of us, especially Herman, whose grandfather had been conscripted into the German navy during World War II.

We'd been the first people to stay aboard since she'd been driven deep into the Everglades by a relentless tidal surge, which some historians say reached twenty feet.

The fact that the submarine had been driven across the barrier islands and more than ten miles into the Glades lent credence to the high water the storm surge had produced.

Roiling water suddenly erupted at the stern of the sub. Then, after a couple of seconds, it stopped.

But the sub was moving forward.

Standing on the observation deck of the conning tower, Rusty turned and waved exuberantly, the smile on his face visible to me half a football field away.

I waved back. "You're under way!"

"See you in Whitewater Bay!" he shouted back.

The sub continued to drift forward and, for the first time since October 19, 1944, the U-320 had moved under her own power.

Not with her original diesel or electric propulsion systems, of course. Rusty had spent a small fortune on replacing the electric motors and batteries.

We knew the day she'd last moved on her own because she'd been driven inland by the storm surge of the Cuba-Florida Hurricane of 1944, which made landfall on Sanibel Island on that date. There was no other plausible explanation for how a submarine could wind up that far inland.

Water splashed at the stern again, this time for a few seconds longer, and then it stopped. That was to be it for the U-320 moving under her own power. At least for the next couple of months.

Replacements for the two diesel engines had been ordered and would arrive in Key West in a couple of months, possibly even before the sub could get there.

A small tug moved toward the U-320's bow as the sub emerged from the muck depression that'd been her berth for more than eight decades. It was a small tug, only twenty-four feet, but small was what was needed.

Its bow contacted the sub, then the tug's powerful engine revved, causing far more water disturbance than the sub's twin props as the little tug nudged the U-320's bow sideways in the newly dug channel.

Digging the channel hadn't taken long. Two barge-mounted excavators had worked day and night for over six weeks digging it, beginning the day after the permits were approved.

They'd created a gouge in the muddy bottom that was twenty

feet deep and more than twice that in width, installing markers along the southern edge of the drop-off.

The new channel extended nearly ten miles toward the coast, but going any further than Whitewater Bay would have to wait until a new lock system could be built to lower the sub the last two or three feet to Big Sandy Creek. The Florida agricultural industry couldn't allow good freshwater to escape South Florida without using most and polluting the rest, so a series of dikes and locks surrounded what was left of the Glades.

Once the lock got built, the sub would be moved into it from Whitewater Bay, where it would sit for another undetermined amount of time, while more dredging in the mouth of Big Sandy Creek created enough depth to get the U-320 into the open Gulf of Mexico, where tugs would then take her to Key West to be decommissioned as a warship.

She still had a deck-mounted anti-aircraft gun forward of the conning tower, though it was frozen in place and covered with rust, rendering it completely inoperable. But the decommissioning process would require its removal, along with any other weapons of war.

There were no torpedoes on board, which we'd found a little odd, and the tubes had actually been welded shut for some reason. Rusty's research revealed that the U-320 had been badly damaged in the North Sea, and all but the captain and a handful of officers had abandoned ship.

The remaining crew had secretly taken the sub to a port for repairs, and she became part of the "rat lines," transporting several wealthy and high-ranking Nazi officers to South America.

As she turned, I could no longer see the tug on the other side. Unlike modern subs, which have almost no deck area above water when operating on the surface, U-boats were built more like ships, floating higher in the water, with a raised bow. So it only needed fifteen-and-a-half feet of water.

The engineers insisted that the channel would begin to fill in with more detritus and mud as soon as the dredging stopped, which was why they'd dredged to twenty feet.

The River of Grass was slow but powerful, and the bottom was a uniform shallow depth for the most part. In time, this dredging scar would be filled in, as if man had never been there.

If only the rest of the Glades could be so fortunate.

Dredging and dike building had started in the late 1800s or early 1900s, depending on whether you were talking about failed attempts or successful ones, but by the mid-1920s, much of what had once been pristine and vibrant wetland habitat had been "reclaimed" for agriculture.

Just how did one reclaim something that was never theirs?

Today, thousands of miles of roads, levees, and canals have altered the natural flow of the Everglades, leaving it less than half the size of what it had once been. Polluted water flowed quickly to designated locks in the levees, disgorging thousands of pounds of toxic chemicals into small areas of the Gulf of Mexico and Florida Bay, which caused massive algae blooms, suffocating fish, reefs, and other animals.

So what was one more ten-mile cut?

The tailings of the dredging operation had been deposited on the upstream or northern side of the canal, to expedite nature's ability to level the bottom once more. But I knew it would take a very long time.

For most rivers, the current is measured in miles per hour. Some great rivers, like the Missouri and Mississippi, flow at three or four miles per hour.

But in the Glades, water flowed at about half a mile per *day*—the speed of mud.

"Did you ever think it would happen?" Savannah asked from the copilot's seat. "Because I had my doubts."

I looked over at her, filming the operation with Billy's digital camera, excited about what we were witnessing. The camera was Wi-Fi enabled, and she was sharing what she recorded through her phone to Rusty and Billy aboard the sub.

Having securely strapped the paddleboard to the float, I climbed into the plane. All three of us had used the board to paddle over to the sub and back.

I propped the door partly open with my foot. "I had my doubts about it moving under its own power," I replied as we watched. "But I never doubted Rusty's ability to recover it."

Rusty Thurman was a wheeler-dealer and long-time salvage operator, as were his father and grandfather before him, and a whole slew of Conch ancestors before them. He had to maintain a number of licenses to be able to legally do some of the salvage work he did, and some of the hoops the state made him jump through, just to add more in the way of unnecessary fees, were ridiculous.

In the state of Florida, to legally salvage anything from the bottom, like a sailboat, skiff, or even something small like a refrigerator or chest, whether it was sunk in offshore or inshore waters, Rusty had to have the same *fishing* license a commercial fisherman would hold, as well as a restricted species endorsement.

Just in case there was a fish in the boat when he re-floated it.

But he maintained every license required, and often said he could pay the fees for all of them, plus the gas and labor involved in the recovery, with just one derelict boat, once he fixed it up and sold it.

Everyone knew Rusty paid a finder's fee, and local fishermen often provided him with the GPS coordinates of possible sunken boats they'd found on fish finders.

Surprisingly, dozens of boats disappeared beneath the waves every year in South Florida, and many were just never reported.

But for *this* salvage operation, there was a necessary license that Rusty didn't have—an archeological research permit. He'd quietly obtained one immediately after Billy found the sub.

"After all this," Alberto said from the backseat, "I sure hope it doesn't sink in the bay."

Knowing that Whitewater Bay was mostly five or six feet deep, I couldn't help but laugh.

"Only the part they dredged is deep enough for it," I said. "If it sinks there, Rusty wouldn't even get his shoes wet on the observation deck."

CHAPTER THREE

Rusty and Billy had waited four months after getting the research permit before reporting the sub as a derelict vessel and applying to the state to recover and remove it.

The location itself was a huge obstacle, leading to miles of red tape from three different entities. Where the sub had come to rest, back in 1944, had been very close to the boundary area between the national park, the state-owned wetlands that were managed by the Southwest Florida Water Management District, and the land belonging to the Seminole Nation.

The current GPS location was on water within the Seminole Reservation, which made the initial decision easy. With Billy leading the way, they quickly agreed to have the vessel moved. But Everglades National Park was between the reservation and the Gulf of Mexico, and dredging ten miles through the park took a lot of convincing.

None of them *wanted* an eighty-year-old, steel submarine rusting away in the Everglades, but all of them wanted to get their share of public recognition for the discovery and to fight the others for control of who fixed things.

In the end, Rusty's long-standing history of successful salvages, coupled with his having all the necessary permits, had won out. If it was to be removed, Rusty was the only one permitted to do it, since he'd been the one who'd filed the initial derelict claim.

Most laws regarding maritime salvage were written in the days of sailing ships and not much had changed. It was basically finders-keepers, and by declaring the sub as a derelict vessel to the Florida Fish and Wildlife Conservation Commission, Rusty automatically held the salvage rights, once they deemed it a derelict.

My daughter Kim, and her husband Marty, both sworn officers and now lieutenants with FWC and having jurisdiction in that area, had done exactly that, and declared the sub a derelict.

That got the ball rolling... also at the speed of mud.

"The fog's lifting," Alberto said. "We can take off pretty soon."

As the sub and tug moved away toward the west, I could see that he was right. More and more of the long, green leaves of sawgrass were appearing as the sun warmed the landscape and the moisture in the air condensed on the leaves to run down to the water.

"They have ten miles to go," I said. "And probably won't reach Whitewater Bay until mid-afternoon. We could be there in just a few minutes."

"What time are Jimmy and Naomi meeting us there?" Savannah asked, stopping the recording.

I looked at my watch. It was 0800.

"He promised to be there by noon," I replied, watching the sub and tug disappear around a cypress head.

"I want to get some high-level video," she said. "Do we have enough gas to circle around for a little while?"

I'd filled the tanks before leaving Marathon, and flying due north for just forty-five miles, we'd gone only about one-tenth of the Beaver's range.

"We can easily fly around for an hour or so," I replied. "Once we're airborne, that is."

We didn't have long to wait as the sun climbed higher into the eastern sky, and the mist subsided even more.

Finally, I stepped back out onto the float and started pulling up the anchor, dropping the line into the storage compartment of the port float as it came up.

When I reached the chain, I pulled it up more slowly, shaking it around to get the mud off. I had to dunk the mushroom anchor a few times. It was covered in the rich, black muck. Then I dropped it on top of the rest of the anchor rode and closed the compartment.

"Ready to take off?" I asked, climbing back in and buckling up.

"Preflight's finished through step three," Savannah said, handing me the laminated card. "Let's get this show on the road."

Island Hopper had sat overnight, and that was plenty long enough to get some oil in the lower combustion chambers. So I turned the engine over with the magnetos off, bumping the starter a quarter revolution at a time, to allow the valves to open and any oil that might have accumulated to drain out.

Then I turned the magnetos on and cranked it again. The big radial engine started easily and, after a couple of coughs and belches of gray smoke, it evened out, and I turned the Beaver in the direction of the long, clear spot I'd landed on the previous day.

There was no wind, so we could take off in any direction, but I already knew the safest bet. I taxied in the direction we'd landed from for several hundred yards, then turned the plane completely around to take off on the same stretch of water I'd landed on.

I knew there weren't any logs there, but a dozing gator could still be a problem. Fortunately, *Island Hopper* had her own alligator warning system.

Her engine.

"All four wheels are up and locked," Savannah advised over my headset. "Four blue lights."

"Roger that," I replied, lowering the flaps for takeoff.

The landing gear built into the Wipaire floats could be retracted into their hulls for water operation or deployed to land on a runway. The indicator lights were simple—green for ground and blue for water.

I pushed the throttle control forward to takeoff speed, and the engine roared in defiance, waking every sleeping gator for a mile around as the agile bird gathered speed.

In less than a hundred yards, the floats came up on their stepped hulls, reducing drag, and after another hundred yards, *Island Hopper* lifted off the water and I pulled back on the yoke and turned in the direction the sub had taken.

At five hundred feet, I eased back on the throttle, leveling off, and reduced flaps as we continued to gain airspeed.

The Beaver's stall speed is very low, just fifty-five miles per hour with the flaps up. With the flaps down, she flies slower than a car on a leisurely drive down a country road.

The sub was less than half a mile ahead, with the little tugboat tied off to the starboard side, aft the conning tower. A trail of disturbed water from the tug's prop extended twice the sub's length behind them.

Rusty was still standing on the observation deck, and Billy and Trish had joined him. Herman was probably down below, doing a post-op on the electric motors and batteries.

Savannah started recording again as I flew low and slow, making a lazy circle around the sub.

"Can you get a little lower on the next pass along the port

side?" she asked, looking down at the sub. "And can you go a little slower?"

I pulled back on the throttle and added flaps as we dropped down to a hundred feet, slowing to just fifty miles per hour, still well above *Hopper's* forty-five-mile-per-hour stall speed with the added lift of the flaps.

As we passed around the stern and started around the port side, I dropped lower, understanding what she was going for. The little tugboat disappeared behind the sub as Savvy filmed a slow pass.

We continued to circle the sub for nearly an hour, with Savannah getting plenty of footage, until finally, we *were* getting low on gas. Not real low, but I preferred getting back to the airport with at least a quarter tank in reserve.

Climbing, I turned toward the sub for one last overhead pass and waggled the wings. Our friends, and even the tugboat crew, waved back as we flew over.

The ten-mile flight to Whitewater Bay took only a few minutes, and I radioed my intention to land on both the aviation band and on the marine VHF channel sixteen, in case there were any bass fishermen out on the bay.

Surprisingly, a familiar voice came over my headset in reply. "*Island Hopper, Island Hopper*, this is *Lunasea*. Do you copy?"

I keyed the mic. "Hey, Jimmy. You're early."

Jimmy Saunders was a close friend and had been my first mate and island caretaker for a very long time. He and his new wife, Naomi, had moved to the mainland last year when I offered to help get them started in oyster farming.

"Just coming across the bar at the mouth of Big Sandy," Jimmy replied. "Had to time the tide, man. Where are you?"

I looked off to the west, and far in the distance, I could see a boat moving into the mouth of Big Sandy Creek, about three miles away.

"I see you," I replied. "I'm at your two o'clock, about three miles out, at three hundred feet, descending to land."

"Cool!" he replied. "We'll see you in a few minutes."

"Lunasea?" Alberto said. "Like the boat Boone and Emily used to have."

"Remember when you told Jimmy about your dives?" I asked. "And how your instructors had to borrow a boat because Emily blew theirs up? He said he really liked the name Lunasea."

"Won't Boone and Emily be mad?" he asked, referring to the instructor couple who'd trained the him and Deuce's boys while we were in the Turks and Caicos.

Savannah turned in her seat and put a finger to her lips. "We just won't tell them."

CHAPTER FOUR

I flew low over the length of Whitewater Bay, which is more of a lake than a bay, checking for boats, debris, or anything else that might be in the way, and saw nothing. So I climbed, banking first to the right, then to the left, to circle around and line up with the patch of water I'd just flown over.

After cutting the power back, I lowered the flaps and pushed the yoke forward slightly, descending toward the water.

"Still four blue lights," Savannah said, confirming that the landing gear hadn't inadvertently been deployed.

She leaned toward me to see the gauges. "Air speed's sixty," she said, then a moment later, "Fifty miles per hour."

I added a little throttle as I flared and set the floats down on the calm water.

Island Hopper quickly slowed, and I turned toward the east side, near the north end, where a set of mooring balls had been anchored for the submarine to wait for the lock to be built.

"There it is," Alberto said, pointing his finger between the front seats. "About 1130."

"There's only 360 degrees on a compass," Savannah said. "That's southeast, so about 1:30… *degrees?*"

"He meant like halfway between eleven o'clock and twelve o'clock," I said with a grin.

Savvy had great navigational skills and better-than-average

natural compass perception, but she struggled to turn that into a clockface to give direction.

I steered toward the two large mooring balls, each a good four feet in diameter, painted yellow, and spaced more than a hundred feet apart.

"I'll go between them and anchor closer to shore," I said. "When the wind comes back it'll be out of the east and will blow us back toward them."

A few minutes later we passed between the mooring balls, and I continued about a hundred yards farther before killing the engine and unlatching my door.

Unfolding myself from the cockpit, I grunted as I lifted one leg out, then the other. *Island Hopper's* cockpit was roomy, as small planes went, but airplane manufacturers don't seem to design aircraft for pilots over six feet tall.

When I stepped down onto the float, I arched my back and stretched. We'd only been in the air for a couple of hours, but it felt good to get out of the plane.

I could hear the sound of an outboard way off to the northwest and looked that way but didn't see anything. I quickly deployed the anchor, letting out about half of the ten feet of chain attached to it before hitting the bottom. It took a full minute as the plane slowly drifted toward the southwest, until the rest of the chain went in.

Little by little, I let out all fifty feet of nylon dock line that was attached to the chain. Then I clipped the carabiner attached to a loop on the end to the cross brace between the floats.

It was way more scope than needed in such shallow water, especially since *Island Hopper* only weighed about three thousand pounds, and I rarely attempted to anchor her in anything deeper than ten feet, so I just used all the rode, all the time.

The rear door opened, Alberto climbed out and pointed. "Is that Jimmy and Naomi?"

Looking in the direction he indicated, I saw a boat approaching about half a mile away. It was a smaller center console with a dark red canvas T-top.

"I think it is," I replied, as Savannah appeared at the rear hatch.

I looked back into the cockpit, then up at her again. "How'd you—"

"Yoga," she replied, before I could finish. "You should try it sometime. It helps with arthritis."

I scowled up at her. "You know I don't—"

"Not yet," she said, cutting me off again and stepping nimbly down to the float. Then she smiled at me. "We're not getting any younger."

Alberto looked around as the approaching boat slowed. "At least we don't have to wait all day in the plane."

As the boat came down off plane and started idling between the two mooring balls, I could see that it was definitely Jimmy and Naomi.

He turned, then reversed the engine as Naomi went forward to hand me the bow line.

I took it, fended the boat away, then quickly tied it off to the float's forward cleat as Savannah did the same with their stern line.

"Great to see you again, *hermano*," Jimmy said, grinning. "Y'all come aboard."

The boat was at least twenty-five feet long, and very wide, carrying close to ten feet of beam from just aft the bow all the way to the stern, making it not really trailerable. At least not without oversized permits.

The helm was set farther aft than is typical for a center

console, and had a well thought-out instrument panel around a twelve-inch multi-display screen. Forward was an expansive open deck space with low gunwales.

The T-top shaded the console, helm area, and the aft deck, which was small but had nicely upholstered seating all the way around.

"Think your anchor will hold us both?" Jimmy asked.

"For now," I replied. "If the wind picks up, we'll probably have to set yours out. Is this your new work boat?"

He grinned. "Sure is, man. Naomi and I built her ourselves. I call it a 'mullet' boat." He smiled at his own joke. "All work up front and party in the back."

I chuckled. "You two built this yourself?"

"With live oak frames and marine plywood," he replied. "Then about four hundred pounds of fiberglass and another two hundred in polyester resin. She's twenty-six feet long, and ten wide." He pointed forward. "See that pedestal in front of the console? I have a davit on order that'll be able to lift a full oyster cage right up on the foredeck, then onto a rolling pallet at the dock."

"Sit down, everyone," Naomi said. "Get comfortable. We have cold drinks if anyone's thirsty."

"Got your favorite, Alberto," Jimmy said, opening a cooler. "A&W root beer."

"Thanks," Alberto said, grabbing a bottle and opening it before taking a seat in the corner. "Have you guys harvested the first oysters yet?"

"In two weeks," Naomi replied, sitting next to him and giving him a quick hug. "I haven't seen you in so long. You've grown."

"I'm over a hundred and ten pounds now," he replied.

"I dove the cages a couple of days ago," Jimmy replied. "Those little one-inch seedlings Carl and Charlie started us out with are now the perfect market size."

The rest of us sat down and Jimmy continued, "So harvesting starts as soon as the crane arrives. Anyway, tell us what happened, man. Did they get the sub out?"

"It's headed this way," I replied. "Probably be around fourteen hundred before they get here, though."

I looked at my watch, surprised to see that it was almost noon. My stomach rumbled.

Savannah glanced at me. "It's almost lunchtime. We have enough sandwiches and snacks on the plane for everyone."

Alberto put his root beer in a cup holder and got to his feet. "I'll get it. Dad would eat half before getting back out of the plane."

CHAPTER FIVE

We had lunch in the shade of the T-top, got caught up on everything that was going on in our lives and in Marathon, then Jimmy broke out a chessboard and challenged Alberto to a game.

The two of them went forward, sat cross-legged on the deck, and used the davit pedestal as a table, while I kicked back and stretched my legs out, letting the sun warm my face as the two women talked.

The gentle rock of the boat, unlimited leg room, and the sound of birds along the shoreline calmed my mind.

Since returning from Venezuela four months ago, I'd been trying to find moments like this, when I just didn't have a thing that needed doing, no important place to be, and no reason to see or speak to anyone I didn't want to.

Living in the moment.

It'd been quite easy to do when we were cruising, especially during a long passage. We'd usually had at least two others on board for most of the year, meaning long passages were broken up into two-hour helm watches, followed by eight hours of down time between shifts. A typical twenty-four-hour period consisted of six hours on and eighteen off. I only slept seven, so those other eleven hours, I was free to indulge myself in a book, or music, or just sit and watch the ocean go by. With no guilt about not doing anything productive.

Soon, my mind drifted to what had happened just a few months ago when one of my crew, Gregor Albert, had been murdered, but the worst part was that the sniper had been shooting at Pete Wadsworth, who was the captain of *Gaspar's Revenge*, my primary charter boat. The assassin mistook Pete for me, and Gregor had stepped into the line of fire.

Just after I'd returned from Venezuela, I'd sent a message, loud and clear, when I'd asked to meet Pablo Lopez, the man who'd shot and killed Gregor. Detective Pine had arranged an interview room and promised not to record.

Lopez had at first been surprised to see me, but with my hair and beard still scraggly, he only recognized me from the dock, when Deuce and I had confronted him before the shooting.

I'd placed the flyer on the table and told him how I'd killed Enrique Alvarez, as well as eight other *sicarios* he'd sent.

"You're the only one that got lucky," I'd quietly growled at him.

I knew the cartel had ways of getting information to and from members who were incarcerated, and I knew that word would get back to the cartel bosses, but more to the point, word would spread to other would-be assassins. Some people were just damned hard to kill.

"Check!" I heard Jimmy exclaim softly, as if in anticipation.

I grinned, my eyes closed.

"Mate," Alberto replied, triumphantly. "That'll be one dollar."

It was a standing rule. Alberto didn't play capable opponents for free and Jimmy was a very good chess player. One dollar was the going bet and Alberto had been putting money away in his sock drawer for a few years.

The radio on Jimmy's dash crackled. "*Lunasea, Lunasea,* this is *Uniform Three Two Zero.* Do you copy?"

I sat up as Jimmy came around the console. It was likely that was the first time in a lifetime that anyone had used the sub's number to call on the VHF.

"*U-Three-Twenty* , this is *Lunasea,*" Jimmy replied into the mic as he looked eastward. "Where are you, man?"

"Them egghead engineers didn't figure on the faster water movement at depth," Rusty said. "We've had a half-knot current behind us for the last six miles. The tug had some trouble a few times, just keepin' us in the channel."

"Leave it to Rusty to give a long, drawn-out reply that doesn't answer the question," I said, getting to my feet.

I looked at my watch. It was almost 1300, five hours since the sub had gotten underway on its ten-mile trek. "An extra half a knot will put them here just about any time now."

I looked toward the east, where the small temporary markers showed where the dredges had deepened the bottom of the inland bay.

Through the trees, I could see movement.

"There he is," I said, spotting the bright white pilothouse of the tugboat and hearing its chugging diesel before seeing the looming hulk of the submarine.

I had to admit, the sight of a World War II German U-boat moving through the trees and sawgrass was unsettling. It didn't belong here. Not in this place or in this time.

"We see you, man," Jimmy said excitedly. "Your mooring balls are all set up."

The tug and submarine moved out of the treeline through a canal that probably destroyed fifteen or twenty mangroves and started toward us at a snail's pace.

The tug's captain kept the sub close to the temporary markers as they began a sweeping turn toward the mooring balls.

"Think we should go over and help?" Jimmy asked.

"The captain knows we're here," I replied. "If he needs help, he'll ask for it."

The tug lined up for the balls and approached at about two knots. Then, just as his boat passed very close to the first one, he reversed his engine, revving it higher.

The sub's bow began to swing to the right as mass and momentum kept it moving forward.

Billy strode toward the bow, passing the anti-aircraft gun, heading to a line that was coiled and ready. He had a long boat hook in hand.

The tug and sub continued forward, slowing as the bow moved to the right. As they slowed to a stop, the tug's engine revs dropped to an idle, and the stern of the sub started moving toward the other mooring ball.

The captain was using "prop walk" to his advantage. Being a single engine, the spinning prop often pulled a boat sideways when it was in reverse.

Rusty moved aft with another boat hook as Billy grabbed the mooring line with his. In just a few minutes, they had the sub tied off with bow and stern lines, plus two spring lines going diagonally.

"Now we can go over," I said, heading to the bow to untie the line.

Jimmy started the engine, a ninety horsepower Suzuki, untied the stern line, then we both pushed away from *Island Hopper's* float.

A couple of minutes later, we tied off to the side of the sub, where Herman lowered a rope-and-wood ladder, known as a "Jacob's" ladder for us.

"Whatta ya think?" Rusty asked, as Jimmy climbed up, then turned to help Naomi.

"Looks real old, man," he replied. "Is that a cannon up there?"

"You betcha," Herman replied, in a distinctive U.P. or "Yooper" accent. "It's an eighty-eight-millimeter naval gun. She also had a thirty-seven-millimeter and two twenty-millimeter anti-aircraft guns, but they'd been removed before setting sail for South America."

"Why'd they do that?" Alberto asked.

"I haven't the foggiest," Herman replied. "Maybe to cut down on weight, eh?"

Rusty smiled. "I think we're gonna call her *Rán*."

"Ron?" I asked. "Who the hell is Ron?"

"Not Ron with an O, ya big ape," Rusty replied. "*Rán*, kinda like drawn without the D. She's the Norse goddess of the ocean and shipwrecks. Me bein' Norwegian, it fits."

"Speaking of Norse goddesses," Jimmy said, as he turned to face Rusty. "Did you ever get the DNA results back?"

"DNA?" I asked.

"Me and Sid did that Ancestry thing," Rusty replied. "Her idea; I know where the Thurmans come from."

Jimmy laughed. "Dude, that's just one branch. Just six generations back, your Grandpa Thurman was one of sixty-four in that generation, and 126 total ancestors, half of which were women."

I nodded at Jimmy. "He's right. You could be more English than anything."

"Bite your tongue," he snapped. "My people *conquered* England over a thousand years ago. Most of Europe too."

CHAPTER SIX

The idea of turning the sub into a tourist attraction was ludicrous, and all Rusty needed was to go out as crew on *Gaspar's Revenge* with Pete to remember why hauling tourists around wasn't much fun. He'd already pushed his social limits by upgrading the bar and restaurant, not to mention the lionfish dinner every Saturday.

My guess would be the best he was going to get on the sub deal was admiration from other salvage operators for pulling it off, and the respect from the maritime community as a whole when he donated it to a public museum.

Rusty had dreams of selling the sub and making a million bucks, but there were only four other German U-boats in existence today. One was in Chicago, a second in Liverpool, England, and two in Germany. All acquired by science or maritime museums through donations or symbolic sales of one Deutsche mark.

I felt pretty sure that Rusty knew all this, but it never stopped the wheeler-dealer in him from dreaming big.

Between now and then? Who knew? The plan was to take the sub to Key West. But there were still several miles of wetland and shallow coastal waters before a sea-going tug could drag *Rán* the last thirty-five miles to the Naval Air Station.

With the sub tied off to the mooring balls, there was little else to be done for a few months until the next part of the dredging and construction of the lock was completed. Both were underway, but the going was slow and plagued with equipment breakdowns.

Until then, Rusty planned to continue to try to rebuild the main diesel engines and get other things back online, like the dive planes and rudder, which were all stuck.

The bow plane on the starboard side was angled downward slightly, which would make the sub want to roll that way when moving forward, and the rudder was turned slightly to port, which made it want to turn away from the roll, making a bad situation even worse and the tug's job much harder.

Herman gave Jimmy and Naomi a short tour of the boat, with the rest of us following along. We had some time to kill before the security people from FWC would arrive. They'd be watching over things during the next several months.

Six hand-picked officers from Florida Fish and Wildlife Conservation Commission would be tasked with watching over the sub in rotating six-hour shifts around the clock, unless Rusty or someone else was there working on it.

Two officers were assigned out of Flamingo, two more from Key Largo, and one each from Marathon and Fort Myers. They typically worked eight-hour shifts, and it would take some of them an hour to get to the remote site.

"And it's just gonna sit here all that time?" Jimmy asked, checking out the new electric motors.

"The water cops will make sure nothin' happens," Rusty said. "And we hope to have at least one of the diesels up and runnin' by the time we put to sea."

Jimmy glanced over at one of the hulking antique diesels. "Yeah, right, man. Where're you gonna source parts for those things?"

Billy smiled. "We're making them. One of my people is a metal worker and we've set up a small furnace and forge in my shop."

"I use a 3-D printer to make the molds," Herman explained. "As each part has been removed, cleaned, and inspected, they've been digitally scanned in case a replacement is needed."

"High-tech science and old-school German engineering, huh?" Jimmy asked. "Very cool."

"When they were new," Herman began, placing a hand on the starboard engine, "each of these *Germaniawerft* F46 powerplants produced one thousand and six hundred metric horsepower."

Rusty winked. "Herman here thinks he can get two thousand horses out of each."

"I don't doubt it, man," Jimmy replied. "Just the advances in super-chargers might do that. How fast will she go?"

"Maximum hull speed on the surface for this vessel is almost twenty knots," Herman replied. "Once both engines are running, that'll be our target, eh? Submerged...? About half that."

"Ten knots underwater," Jimmy said softly, then looked over the engine at Rusty. "Dude, it needs some viewing ports."

"Windows on a submarine?" Naomi asked.

Rusty chuckled. "We were thinkin' of that. Them torpedo tubes would fit the bill. As long as you ain't too claustrophobic."

"Observation ports in the torpedo tubes?" I asked dubiously.

"Why not?" Rusty replied. "Part of the process of decommissionin' her will be sealin' up the tubes anyway, so why not cover the outer doors with thick glass and remove most of the tubes on the inside? But so far, we haven't been able to even open 'em."

"No torpedoes on board?" Jimmy asked. "Only one gun?"

"We think the boat was being used to transport high-ranking Nazi officers to South America," Herman replied. "I'm still trying to decipher the captain's logbook, eh. They didn't need torpedoes because the tubes were welded closed, inside and out. Probably as a precaution with an undermanned crew."

"They didn't want one of them Nazi generals to push the wrong button and flood the whole torpedo room," Rusty added, then turned to me. "The tubes look like they're about twenty-four inches wide, so maybe not for everyone."

Through the hull we could hear the tugboat's engine starting, getting ready to head home.

"I can fit inside a two-foot tube," I said, as we started for the ladder to the conning tower.

"That's OD, bro," he said, climbing up first. "Them tubes gotta be just as thick as the hull plates, three-quarters of an inch. I bet we won't find much more'n twenty-one inches of *inside* diameter."

CHAPTER SEVEN

After the tugboat left, we waited another half hour before two FWC boats entered the bay from the northwest. They started toward us, on plane and running side by side.

As they got closer, I recognized my middle daughter, Kim, at the helm of one, and her husband Marty standing in the bow, leaning back with one hand on the bow line while watching for shallows or floating objects. The men in the other boat were doing the same.

I checked my watch. It was 1400, and they were right on time.

Once they slowed and got close enough, Rusty shouted, "Come around and tie off to the mooring balls!"

A few minutes later, I was hugging Kim and shaking Marty's hand. Then they introduced the other two men, Phil Mahoney and Bruce Sinclair.

Rusty shook hands with the two officers, then turned to Marty. "I appreciate y'all helpin' out. There'll be some days over the comin' months when we'll have people workin' out here, and I'll let you know a few days ahead, so you don't have to waste manpower."

Kim glanced over at the hulking submarine for a moment, then looked back at Rusty. "Getting *that* out of *here* is a top priority for FWC right now. We're glad to help."

Marty faced the two officers. "It's an easy gig, guys. But if you're out here at night, it'll be buggy."

"I got just the thing for that," Jimmy said, moving aft toward his boat. A moment later he was back, carrying a kerosene lantern and a one-gallon can. "If you put this up on the bow and tie your boat off to the stern, it'll keep most of the bugs busy. A gallon's all I got, but it'll last at least two nights."

"That'll do the trick," Rusty said, "but set it up there from your boat. There can't be no boardin' unless I'm here. The hatches'll be locked."

"What if there's an emergency?" Mahoney asked.

"Still no boardin'," Rusty said. "Too dangerous. That's why the watertight hatches are locked. This is an eighty-one-year-old steel ship and it's been sittin' out here rustin' for most of that time. Even if it sinks, the hatch on the observation deck'll still be above water. I just don't want nobody gettin' hurt."

"Consider it done, sir," the second officer, Sinclair, said.

Other than him having blue eyes and the other, brown, they might have been twins. Same height, build, hair color, and features.

"Don't worry," Kim said. "These guys are used to overnight stakeouts on the water."

"All our guys are," Sinclair added. "At least what we're watching this time isn't a poacher or swamp chemist."

That was a new one on me. "Swamp chemist?"

"Meth labs deep in the Glades," Mahoney said.

Rusty gave me a furtive glance. The kidnappers of his cousin, Madison, had been meth lab operators in another swamp up in Apalachicola.

"Not to worry," Mahoney added, seeing his expression. "They tend to scurry *away* from lights."

"We oughta get goin'," Rusty said, turning to me. "How long is it back to Marathon?"

"Forty-five minutes, once we're in the air."

Billy turned and looked toward the south. "I hear our ride coming."

At the far end of the bay, an airboat appeared around a cypress head, turned toward us, and accelerated. There was a lone figure perched on the upper seat.

"That's my neighbor's kid, Danny," Billy said, turning toward me and offering a hand. "Don't be a stranger."

We shook hands as the airboat slowed. I recognized it as Billy's.

"Yes," Trish said to Savannah. "Maybe you can come up next weekend for a cookout? We have a landing strip in the backyard now."

Savvy looked at me and I nodded. "Let's do it. What can we bring?"

"Just your appetites," Billy said with a smile. "I'll start the smoker before sunup."

"We'll be there shortly after," I said. "Sounds like fun."

Jimmy stepped down into his boat and started the engine, then helped Naomi down.

The rest of us boarded as the airboat came alongside us, the prop feathered. The kid at the stick looked vaguely familiar as he climbed down, and Billy stepped up to the elevated driver's seat.

As we idled the short distance to *Island Hopper*, Trish and Billy both waved. "See you next Sunday," he shouted.

Then the airboat's engine roared, and they were off, Billy's long ponytail trailing behind him.

When we reached the plane, I stepped up and opened both

hatches on the port side. Alberto climbed in and went up to the cockpit to open the hatch on the other side.

"Appreciate your help," Rusty said to Jimmy. "It woulda been real uncomfortable sittin' in the plane for this long." Then he nodded at Naomi. "Both of ya. Sid said to tell ya to come down Saturday if ya can."

"Don't mention it, man," Jimmy said. "We've been wanting to see that thing for a while. And it's always good to catch up."

We said our goodbyes, and they promised to make it down one weekend for Rusty and Sid's "Lionfish Safari." Then Jimmy motored slowly back around the sub as I pulled up the anchor.

When I climbed in, Savvy handed me the checklist. "All through," she said.

I glanced at the switches and gauges, turned on the magnetos and started the engine. It fired up quickly and evenly, with very little smoke, having only been shut down for a short time.

I lowered the flaps as I turned toward the far end of the bay.

Jimmy came around the sub, a hundred feet away, grinning at me.

"Four blue lights," Savannah said, as I reached for the throttle.

When I moved it to the full power setting, the engine roared, and Jimmy mashed the throttle on his boat.

The flat-bottomed boat accelerated quickly, getting on plane in just a few yards, then rocketing ahead a good thirty yards.

Island Hopper's floats came up on the steps, and she gathered speed, rapidly overtaking, then passing, Jimmy and Naomi's boat.

The air over the wings lifted the floats higher, and we broke free of the water, climbing into a beautiful blue sky. I turned toward the east, flying over ancient bald cypress trees as we circled back around toward the sub.

Kim and Marty were on their boat, and both turned to wave as we flew over. Just ahead, Jimmy and Naomi did the same.

I rocked the yoke back and forth, banking the plane from side to side, then turned due south, climbing, and heading for Marathon.

CHAPTER EIGHT

When we reached a thousand feet, I leveled off and glanced back at Rusty, sitting behind Savannah. "You never did say if you got the DNA results back."

"I did," he replied. "And of course, it's all messed up."

"What do you mean?" Savannah asked. "It's science."

"He doesn't believe in science," Sid said with a laugh.

"Science my... butt," Rusty replied. "Okay, so both me and Pop were only children." He paused and leaned forward in his seat. "So I got no first cousins on that side. Mom had a brother who never got married until late in life, and didn't have no kids. So no first cousins there either."

"Well you already knew *that*," Savannah said, becoming intrigued. "How is it messed up?"

"I got a second cousin on Pop's side who lives down on Ramrod," he explained.

"You know her," Sid said. "Michelle Marsh."

"Anyway," Rusty continued, "she did this DNA thing too, and accordin' to the website, she's a three percent match."

"That sounds right to me," I said. "A first cousin would be around a twelve percent match, if my math's right."

"Zactly!" he exclaimed, snapping his fingers. "So why's there someone on there with a *fourteen* percent match who I never heard of?"

"Huh! That's kind of a mystery," Alberto said. "Does it say where the person lives? In the Keys?"

"Not even close," Rusty replied. "Accordin' to his bio on the site, he was born in Central Florida, grew up in Iowa but lives in Illinois now."

I considered the numbers with what little knowledge I had on the subject. I knew we got half of our DNA from each of our parents, so a mother, father, son, or daughter would be a fifty percent DNA match, and grandparents and grandkids would be twenty-five percent, with twelve-and-a-half percent coming from each grandparent. Someone who has two of four grandparents in common with someone else is a first cousin.

People with two of *eight* great-grandparents in common, mathematically, would be a fourth of a first cousin's match, or about three percent, just like Rusty's second cousin, Michelle.

"If I didn't know the players," I said, "and just used the math, it sounds like this person shares grandparents with you on one side, and second great-grandparents on the other. Or maybe first great-grandparents on both sides."

"The latter would be more likely," Rusty replied. "Like I said, Pop had no siblings, and Mom's only brother, my Uncle Chuck, never had any kids. He adopted one, though."

"Is there a way to contact this person?" Savannah asked. "Alberto's right. It does sound like a mystery."

"Speaking of mysteries," Rusty said, leaning forward again and tugging at my sleeve. "Remember that ghost ship you told me about... around six years ago?"

"When I was almost crushed in a glass bubble?" I asked.

Sidney leaned in between the seats. "I haven't heard this one."

"It was when I first hooked up with Armstrong," I replied. "Six years ago. We uncovered an illegal hazardous waste dump site, and I went down with *Ambrosia's* submersible pilot, John Wilson, to check it out. Long story short, there was a leak, John lost an eye, and during the emergency ascent, I saw the wreck of a very old sailing ship."

"Like a treasure ship?" Sid asked.

"Maybe from that period," I replied, looking at her reflection in the mirror. "I didn't get much of a look, though."

"A few weeks back," Rusty began, "I came across the GPS numbers you gave me and started doin' some diggin'."

I looked up in the mirror again. "Six *years* later?"

"Risk versus profit," Rusty stated. "That's the way any salvor looks at things. You said the wreck was over six hundred feet down and I didn't have no way to do that."

When I looked up at the mirror again, he grinned.

"But I do now," he said.

Over the last six years, I'd wondered about the wreck I'd seen but hadn't thought much of it in a while. Who sailed her? What was her name? How did she sink? What cargo did she carry?

I'd only gotten a couple of glimpses of the wreck as the submersible spun wildly during the emergency ascent. The lights attached to the submersible had created a dizzying display on the bottom.

The location was twenty miles out from the Port of Miami, almost halfway to Gun Cay in the Bahamas. It was far beyond the continental shelf, which is very narrow just off Miami, and on the eastern edge of the Gulf Stream, twenty miles from the Bahama Banks.

"I narrowed it down to a little over a hundred possible ships," Rusty said. "There's a lot more'n that down there, but I only concentrated on pre-twentieth century ships headed north and lost at sea."

"The trade routes?" I asked. "Any ship that didn't make port would be reported lost anywhere along that route, but could be anywhere from Florida to Maine, or across the northern Atlantic."

"Yeah," Rusty said. "Unless there was a survivor who could pinpoint where their ship went down. Five of a hunert and seven were firsthand reports by survivors. Those five definitely went down off the South Florida coast."

"Why only ships headed north?" Alberto asked.

"The location's in the Stream," Rusty replied. "Ships headed south would hug the coast to stay outta the current and take advantage of whatever countercurrents might exist. That's why they's so many up around Cape Hatteras."

"The Graveyard of the Atlantic," I added.

"That's a lot of shipwrecks," Alberto said. "How can it be narrowed down?"

"Just like I said," Rusty replied. "We gotta go down and have a look-see. How a ship's built and what it looks like could give us a time period, and maybe even a name."

"Using a rusty, eighty-year-old submarine?" Savannah asked, incredulously. "That's insane."

"Well... we'd have to do a complete systems refit and have the hull ultrasound-tested. It might take a couple of years."

"And a couple million dollars," I said. Then, without thinking, I added, "Why not just buy a submersible?"

"That's right," Alberto said. "*Taranis* was designed to be a mother ship, so it could provide electricity and air for a small submersible."

"You built it to be a submersible tender?" Rusty asked.

"Not exactly," I replied. "But when I started designing her

during the Covid lockdown, that shipwreck was fresh in my mind. I just never removed the hardware from the design."

"What's one of them submersibles cost?" Rusty asked.

I chuckled. "Starting price is around two mil, brother."

"I don't suppose used ones come on the market very often," he grumbled.

I laughed again. "Not with a valid Carfax report on recent accidents, they don't."

CHAPTER NINE

Going back down to that shipwreck I'd stumbled on was an interesting idea. I was the only one who knew about it, and I'd only told a small handful of people. Rusty was the only one I'd given the GPS location to. Revisiting it was something way down on my bucket list, due to the cost involved.

But rather than *buying* a submersible, I wondered if there were any just sitting around collecting dust that could be *rented*. Barring that, taking on a partner that had one and could keep their mouth shut would be the only other alternative. Past experience told me those people were few and far between.

But I did know a few people who operated submersibles, and one of them would soon be close by. *And* he was trustworthy.

Stuart McCormick and I had served together a couple of times during my later years in the Corps. He'd been a PFC assigned to my platoon in 1994, and later, just before I retired, he'd been a sergeant on his second tour, and had been assigned to Weapons Company, Second Reconnaissance Battalion.

He'd retired as a master gunnery sergeant about eight years ago after twenty-four years in the Corps and soon moved into civilian commercial dive operations and submersibles.

If I was going to look into this, that was who I'd start with to see if I could locate a submersible to rent or borrow, or if nothing else, what he'd charge to go down to that deep location in the Gulf Stream.

Not that buying one was *completely* out of the question. When I'd first arrived in the Keys, I had an inheritance that would have lasted a lifetime, living the "normal" subdivided, suburban neighborhood existence. Mowing the lawn on Monday, washing the cars on Tuesday, Wednesday shopping, taking the trash to the curb, trimming the bushes, painting, roofing, remodeling, PTA meetings, community outreach volunteer work, town councils... not to mention the pills on Tuesday and Thursday for the heart and liver.

We'd lived a much simpler life, with our schedule revolving around the sun, moon, and tide. I considered that to be a good investment.

Another good investment was with Rusty. When I'd first retired, it was cool to be the silent partner in his vision, and we helped one another accomplish our dreams. Plus I got to eat and drink for free during my crazy years right after leaving the Corps. He'd even put me up in a guest room until I'd found *Gaspar's Revenge* and moved aboard.

I'd also managed to save a pretty good chunk of change as an enlisted Marine over a twenty-year career, most of which was when I was single and living on base for free.

When I'd bought the *Revenge* and my island, I'd nearly depleted my liquid assets, which was pretty much all the assets I'd had besides a few clothes and uniforms. Even the car I'd driven down in had been a rental.

But I'd done pretty well as a charter boat owner-operator, added scuba diving and photography options, as well as buying other boats to cater to Gulf and Backcountry anglers.

And over the years, I'd found a few bright, shiny things of my own.

In the early days, living alone on my boat, then later, on the island, everything was cheap, even compared to home prices in the Keys back then. My home was paid for, I had no utility bills, and caught a good bit of what I ate.

I'd made some good investments in both the business and people.

Rusty had paid me off in one lump sum not long after I'd arrived, and I didn't have to worry financially.

Savannah's circumstances were similar. When her mother passed away, she'd inherited what her father had left—the proceeds from the sale of his fishing fleet up in Beaufort, South Carolina. She'd also lived most of her adult life on her boat, *Sea Biscuit*, a fifty-foot Grand Banks trawler.

None of our kids would ever *have* to work, but they all did.

I'd spent well over two million building *Taranis*, and she was fully set up with high-pressure air pumps to fill scuba tanks, and two generators for electricity. The only thing she was missing was about a thousand feet of air and electric umbilical, and the submersible. But the connections were already built into the starboard ama.

As we began our descent toward Marathon International, I looked back at Rusty over my shoulder.

"If you're game to give it a try," I said, "it'd be cool to have a small submersible aboard *Taranis*."

Savannah's head snapped around. "Are you out of your mind?"

"We'd use it mostly for shallow dives on reefs," I said, a bit defensively. "A hundred feet, max. Think about it. *Taranis* in auto-station keeping, while you and I cruise along the reef wall completely dry."

"Were you completely dry when you got out of that thing the first time?"

When *Ambrosia's* submersible developed the leak, the water level inside had risen quickly, streaming in through the crack at high pressure, and it'd almost reached my knees in just over a minute before I'd gotten the pump turned on. When I'd climbed out, I was soaked with seawater and John Wilson's blood.

"These things have come a long way in six years," I replied without answering her question. "And that one John and I were in was five years old. That's like... 2014 technology."

"It's probably just some old cargo schooner," she muttered, but I knew she liked the idea.

"A moonlit night," I said. "We could sit on the bottom between finger reefs and watch the sharks."

Savannah loved night diving and, although she burned through air faster than a novice diver whenever we encountered sharks, she said she loved diving with them.

I leveled off, lowered the flaps, and reduced power as we descended over the markers. My hangar was at the far end, so I had lots of runway.

I looked over and Savannah smiled. "I could get used to that."

Once we were down and had *Island Hopper* pushed back into the hangar with her big sister, *Ocean Hopper*, the five of us walked out to the small parking lot where my truck was parked in the hot sun.

"Leave the doors open for a minute," I cautioned, as I reached in with the fob in my hand and pressed the starter button.

The diesel engine started instantly, and I let it run for a few seconds while I pushed the buttons to put all the windows down before turning on the AC.

It was December, but we were in the Keys and *The Beast*, with her leather interior, had been absorbing heat from the sun through her dark brown surface rust all morning.

"You're serious about gettin' a submersible?" Rusty asked through the truck's open doors.

"It's a big investment," I said, getting in. "And Savvy might be right. It could be just a wrecked schooner carrying cotton or something, and besides, like I said, it'd be mostly for fun."

"A very expensive toy," Savannah said, "with another very expensive toy to support it."

Rusty chuckled. "Yeah, well, havin' one available would open up a few *other* sites I know about, too," he said, as he, Alberto, and Sid climbed into the backseat. "Places too deep to dive, but not deep at all for a submersible."

Checking *The Beast's* gauges and finding everything normal, I put her in reverse and backed out of the parking spot, then headed toward the exit.

"How big are these things?" Savannah asked.

"Not big," Alberto replied. "I remember Dad told me it's why *Taranis* has a ten-thousand-pound dinghy davit on the roof and a dinghy garage under the cockpit. The davit's for a two-man sub that can reach a thousand feet."

"Can we test drive one?" she asked.

"I doubt it," I replied, driving out of the airport. "But I know where we can go look at one and learn some more."

"Pompano Beach," Alberto said, looking up from his phone. "A company called America SubDive has two of them, *Voyager* and *Nomad*."

I turned right onto Overseas Highway and immediately got over into the left lane.

"We don't have to go that far," I replied. "One of the SubDive teams has been working down in the Caymans and is being moved up to the oil rigs in the northern Gulf to do some inspections next week."

"And what?" Savannah asked, still not convinced. "We're just going to take *Taranis* up there, wait for them to surface, and ask for a joy ride?"

While waiting for traffic to clear so I could make the U-turn, I looked over at her and grinned. "One of the guys doing the inspecting is a buddy of mine from the Corps."

CHAPTER TEN

Savannah always seemed to find it odd that I knew so many people from my time in the Corps, but she never fully considered the turnover rate. Just in my last five years, I was the battalion range chief and marksmanship instructor, as well as being the company gunny. Every week, it seemed, someone was transferring out, either to another assignment, or back to civilian life, and for each one leaving, the battalion got a replacement.

"Did you know *everyone* in the Marine Corps?" she asked.

"Quite a few," I replied. "Several thousand, at least."

Just during that five-year-period alone, I'd probably met over a thousand Marines for the first time, from privates to sergeants, for the most part. But all came through my range within a month of reporting.

I didn't care how they did on someone else's rifle range; I wanted to see them in action, talk to them, and get to know them. One in a hundred might be a candidate for the scout/sniper platoon.

I made the U-turn, bouncing over the curb on the other side, then slowed immediately for the right into Rusty's place.

The car behind us honked. So I slowed a little more and *The Beast* barely crept onto the crushed shell driveway, like I was driving a Prius and afraid of hurting the suspension.

I waited for a second impatient horn blast, which would have brought *The Beast* to a full stop. She was a fifty-two-year-old International Travelall, with raised suspension, oversized all-terrain tires, and massive tubular steel bumpers that would make even the most intolerant drivers reconsider.

No second honk came.

It darkened as the over-arching live oaks and casuarinas enveloped *The Beast*, and the air coming through the open windows felt noticeably cooler, so I turned off the AC.

"Do you think you can arrange for us to see one while they're up there working on the oil rigs?" Savannah asked.

"Better than that," I replied. "Their transport ship will come to Key West to check into the country before heading up there."

"When?" Savannah asked, as we rounded a curve and I saw Cindy Lee pushing her bike toward us.

"Stop a sec," Rusty said.

I stopped and turned to Savannah. "Actually, they're due to arrive some time tonight, I think."

"Hi," Cindy said, lifting a hand and smiling.

"Everything okay at the bar?" Rusty asked her.

"Oh, yeah," she replied. "Maddy helped me out for the last hour."

Rusty leaned past Alberto. "I thought she was takin' the week off."

Cindy shrugged. "I think the guy canceled."

"What guy?" Rusty asked. "She told me she was goin' over to The Bahamas with a friend."

Dropping her chin and cocking her head slightly, Cindy gave him a questioning look. "Girls have guy friends too, you know."

"A'ight, then," he muttered. "Me and Sid'll be here, but if you wanna, you can come on in and help out with the breakfast bunch."

"Thanks," she said with a smile. "I'll see you in the morning, then."

I knew Cindy was struggling, and so did Rusty. He and Sid could handle the breakfast crowd, which was mostly a few liveaboards, fishing guides, and maybe a client or two.

Cindy would find *something* to do, even if it was just cleaning a spotless bar. She was too proud to accept a handout, and worked every chance she got, either at the Anchor, over at Dockside, or across Boot Key Harbor at Burdines Waterfront.

She was a single mom of two, and shared a tiny four-bedroom house over on Big Pine Key with another single mom.

The Keys needed hard-working people like Cindy and Mona, but housing was the biggest problem for the working class. There wasn't enough of it, and what was available was far too expensive. It was likely the women were paying over $4,000 a month in rent.

I glanced back at my friend, knowing that he'd done the same with dozens, if not hundreds of other locals. Rusty offered a hand *up*, not a handout.

As she walked her bike toward the road, I continued into the parking area and backed in under the live oak where I always did. As everyone piled out, I put the windows up and shut off the engine.

"What do *you* think, Alberto?" Savannah asked. "Your dad wants to blow your inheritance."

He smiled broadly. "Will I get the submersible?"

Sid laughed, then she and Savannah started toward the door. "I tell you, Savvy, the only difference between men and boys is the price of their toys."

We didn't stick around the Anchor for long. It was only 1630 when we arrived, but nightfall was already approaching, and we wanted to be home by sunset.

So we said our goodbyes, and Rusty agreed to go with us the next morning to Key West, if I could get the okay from my friend.

As it was, the sun was barely above the horizon when we reached the dock back at my island, and Larry and Lauren were already sitting there, a small cooler beside them.

Tank stood at the end of the pier, saggy jowls pulled back in a dog smile as he panted with excitement, wagging his huge tail. It had been our first night away from him in a long time.

"I didn't think you were going to make it in time," Larry said, getting to his feet as we idled up.

"It's been a long day," I said, reversing the engine for a second as Alberto handed the bow line to him.

"Did they get it moving?" Lauren asked.

"They certainly did," Savannah said. "And drove it ten miles through the swamp to Whitewater Bay. I took tons of video."

I stepped over with the stern line, quickly cleated it, and helped Savannah out of the boat. Not that she *needed* help, but because she liked the gesture.

Tank moved between us, allowing both of us to rub his ears and flank as he rolled his hips onto my feet.

"Who's a good boy?" Savvy cooed, cupping his big head in her hands.

Lauren opened the cooler and handed Savannah a wine glass, then passed a root beer to Alberto and a Red Stripe to me before uncorking a wine bottle and filling Savannah's glass half full.

"Thanks," I said, as we all sat down on the pier. "Everything go okay, your first night alone on the island?"

"We weren't alone," Lauren replied, draping an arm over Tank's shoulder. "This big guy slept right at the foot of our bed."

"And Mac and Mel came over before sunset and stayed for a while," Larry added. "Did you ask them to do that?"

I looked at him openly, shaking my head. "It never would have occurred to me. What did they want?"

"Mac said your island blocks his view," Lauren said, looking over her shoulder toward Mac and Mel's island, a mile up Harbor Channel.

I glanced back also. I'd never thought of it, but she was right. Over the next three weeks, the sunset would move a little more toward the south, and their island would still be in the shadow of ours, and probably would be until early spring.

"We should extend a standing invitation for happy hour," Savannah suggested.

"An *occasional* offer," I agreed. "But I don't know about an open invitation."

She bumped my shoulder with hers. "You're such a curmudgeon."

I leaned forward, looking past her at Larry. "We might be going down island tomorrow. You're off and Lauren's working. Want to come along?"

"Key West?" he asked. "What for?"

"To look at a submersible Dad's gonna buy," Alberto replied. "To dive on a *pirate* ship in the middle of Florida Straits."

"Seriously?" Lauren asked, surprised.

"There's a wreck there," I said. "What *kind* is unknown. I saw it once, about six years ago, while researching a hazardous waste dump site in a submersible."

"How deep?" Larry asked.

He was an avid scuba diver and had recently been certified as a divemaster, so he could help Pete and Reggie on the dive charters during the coming winter season.

I still hadn't found a replacement for Gregor Albert.

"Close to seven hundred feet," I replied. "It looked like it was wedged in a trench that fell from the edge of the Bahama Banks into the deeper part of the Straits."

He let out a low whistle. "That's in the twilight zone, man."

At seven hundred feet, there isn't enough light for photosynthesis, and the human eye can't detect any light at all at half that depth. It's called the dysphotic or mesopelagic zone, but commonly referred to as the twilight zone.

"Twenty-two atmospheres of pressure," Alberto said. "That's deep."

"But that's not the only reason I'd get one," I said, looking toward the setting sun. "We'll mostly use it for recreation, and Rusty has a few sites he wants to check out that are too deep for scuba."

As the big orange ball seemed to come in contact with the waters of the Backcountry flats, its bottom began to slowly flatten out, a distortion caused by reflection and the extreme angle of the sun's rays through our atmosphere.

"It'd be cool to have a sub," Lauren said. "Just sit on the bottom beside a reef and watch all the fish. You could even talk and have lunch."

At times, my curiosity flared out of control. I loved adventure, as did Savannah. There was always something else to see out there where the sun goes down. But so far, we'd only scratched the surface and gone down to about a hundred feet with scuba or rebreathers.

Savvy had been that deep a few times, and I'd been to two hundred on mixed gas. But Alberto's deepest dive on scuba had only been sixty feet, or ten fathoms.

With a mini-submersible, we could go down as deep as a thousand feet—167 fathoms below sea level.

The twilight zone.

CHAPTER ELEVEN

The sun was slipping below the horizon, and I could feel Savannah's eyes on *me* instead of on the spectacle of light we came out to the pier to witness just about every evening. Since our return, it'd marked the end of the workday, regardless of what day of the week it was, and a time to relax and unwind.

Sunsets had always been popular with us, but lately Savannah seemed to add a degree of necessity to it. She said it was cathartic and grounding, whatever that meant.

"It's just my curious nature, babe," I said softly, without turning to face her. "I saw it, sitting almost upright in a rocky crevice. The hull, rig, and shape were unmistakably eighteenth century, maybe earlier. The foremast was snapped off just above the lower yard arm with the mizzen leaning to starboard. The broken part of the rig hung that way too, with the broken foremast smashing through the toe rail and deck timbers."

"And you want to know why," Savvy said gently. "Well, okay. But I still want that romantic night dive. How long can it stay down?"

When I looked over at her, the sun was full on her face, her features soft and radiant as she watched the sun go down. She looked exactly like the woman I'd met more than twenty years earlier.

Her expression changed to one of awe and I looked back just in time to catch the last little droplet of the sun disappear below the horizon.

"Some of them can stay down a long time," Alberto said, getting to his feet with Tank. "But I think the ones we'll be looking at have a six-hour limit. I'm hungry."

"Everything's ready," Lauren said. "Larry and I put together a boil."

Savannah looked over at her. "A Lowcountry boil?" she asked the younger woman. "With shrimp and sausage?"

Lauren nodded emphatically. "Larry stopped and got everything after work, and I found a recipe online."

"We called it Frogmore stew back home," Savannah said, as I gave her a hand up.

"Frogmore?" Alberto asked.

"It's a little town on St. Helena Island, two islands over from Beaufort, where I'm from. They and dozens of others comprise the Lowcountry Sea Islands."

"One of which is *Parris* Island," I said. "Where I went to boot camp and later served as a drill instructor."

As Lauren and Savannah led the way, with Alberto and Tank bounding ahead, Larry held back, walking slowly. I matched his pace, thinking he had something on his mind.

When the others rounded the corner of the house, he stopped and turned to face me. "Would it be okay if one of the kids from school came out here to stay with me and Lauren for a while?"

"Over crowding problem again?"

"Not exactly," he replied. "Just a kid who needs a little help."

I looked ahead to where Alberto was throwing a large stick for Tank to fetch. "I don't see why not. You do have that extra room."

"Thanks," he said, then turned and followed the others.

I had a feeling I knew who he was talking about. Some months ago, Lauren had told me about one of the students who Larry suspected had been molested. I figured he'd tell me in his own time.

We served ourselves from a simmering pot, then went to the ancient fire ring, where we sat and ate with our fingers from wooden bowls, a Lowcountry tradition, according to Savvy.

"You said the ship you saw was mostly intact?" Larry asked me from across the fire. "With part of the rig standing?"

"I know what you're thinking," I said, and I'd considered a lot of possibilities. "It's deep. Too deep for plant life. But not too deep to be oxygen-deprived."

He held up a shrimp tail and said, "Shipworms," before popping it in his mouth.

"It shouldn't have been that intact," I conceded. "It's not too deep to escape wood borers."

"Which makes it all the more curious for you," Savannah said with a smile. "Maybe it's a recent wreck of a replica ship. I saw an exact copy of Columbus's ship, *Niña*, the last time I was home before Daddy died."

I nodded, savoring the mix of flavors with each bite. "That's a possibility." Then I winked at Lauren. "This is the best Frogmore stew I've ever had."

She smiled.

"There are a lot of reasons an older ship could still be intact," Larry began. "That is, if it's as old as you think. That depth is beyond photosynthesis, yeah, so there's no plant life, and few boring organisms would exist, but probably enough to turn a wooden ship into sand, given two hundred years. It's right at the edge of oxygen deprivation too. Levels are lower, but not so low as to prevent wood borers altogether."

"If it's close to two or three hundred years old," I said, "even at that depth, there shouldn't be that much left."

"Except it's in the Gulf Stream," Alberto suggested. "And you said it was wedged in a trench that went down to deeper water."

"Caused by erosion?" Larry asked rhetorically, pausing with a piece of sausage halfway to his mouth. "Most trenches in the sea floor of a continental shelf are made by water runoff when sea levels were a lot lower. But that deep, it's sure to have been carved by an underwater current."

Alberto handed a shrimp to Tank, who gobbled it down. "Those kinds of currents that last for a long, long time are usually caused by differences in either temperature or salinity."

Alberto was right. Colder water, or water with a lower salinity would tend to sink to the bottom. If whatever conditions caused it to be colder or more saline were to remain for a long time, the "heavier" water could cut canyons just like on land.

"That could be it, buddy," Larry said. "Either a cold-water current, or more saline could further mitigate the abundance and metabolism of shipworms."

"Did you ever contact your friend?" Savannah asked me. "You said they're arriving tonight."

Stuart and I had exchanged a few emails when he learned he'd be up this way, but we hadn't made any definite plans.

I scrolled through the small number of emails on my phone until I found his, then opened it and clicked *Reply*.

After typing a quick note, asking if they were still scheduled to be in the area, I hit *Send*.

"Just did," I replied to Savannah, putting my phone away.

It dinged before I got my hand out of my pocket and I pulled it back out again and looked at the screen.

"That was quick," I said, opening Stuart's reply and reading it.

Then I looked over at Savannah. "He says they're arriving before sunrise and plan to remain there for the whole week, until the oil rigs are ready."

I replied to the email, asking if we could come aboard to look at *Voyager* and *Nomad*, and check out the operation.

When I tapped *Send* again, I watched the screen, waiting to see if he replied just as quickly.

When the phone rang, it startled me. I tapped *Accept* and held it to my ear. "McDermitt."

"Hi, Jesse!" Stu said. "I figured since we both had our phones in our hands…"

Stuart McCormick was originally from Atlanta, Georgia but currently worked and lived in Fort Lauderdale. He had a slight, homey kind of accent that would cause most to initially think he was nothing more than an uneducated hick. But any lengthy discourse would prove that notion false in a hurry.

"Good to hear from you, Stu," I replied, looking around the fire at the others. "How've you been?"

"I can't complain," he replied. "Besides, who'd listen? So you want to check out our subs, huh?"

"If it's possible," I replied.

"We're not doing much of anything tomorrow and Wednesday," he suggested. "We should dock at 0600 and we'll clear in, using CBP's ROAM app. But we'll probably be under quarantine until someone gets to the Customs office to approve our entry. Any time after 0900 should be good."

"I thought the ROAM app was more for civilian use," I said. "Not for commercial vessels.

U.S. Customs and Border Patrol had developed a computer app for people arriving into the country from overseas, and in typical government fashion, chose a catchy acronym for it, Reporting Offsite Arrival–Mobile, or ROAM.

It was especially convenient for people arriving by private vessels in Key West. Customs, Immigration, and Border Patrol were all located at the airport, on the far side of the island from where the marinas, piers, and anchorages were located.

"It is," he replied. "We're classified as a private vessel. Only the submersibles, *Voyager* and *Nomad*, are commercial."

"Can I bring someone?" I asked. "My wife and son, and a couple of friends? One's another jarhead."

"The more the merrier," he replied. "Like I said, tomorrow's a down day, and Wednesday will be mostly the same. Plan on stayin' a few hours and we can have lunch in the galley. Our cook's really good."

"I'm pretty sure we can do tomorrow," I said.

"Good!" Stu exclaimed. "The rest of the week, we'll be up to our asses in alligators, with more of our crew arrivin' and we'll be preppin' for the dives, the first of which has a base at three hundred meters."

"We'll be there by 0900," I replied, then we said goodbye, I ended the call, and looked at Savvy. "We're all set."

"You're going to buy a submersible, aren't you?" she asked.

"Not tomorrow," I replied with a half grin. "We're just going to *look* at a couple."

CHAPTER TWELVE

A week after receiving the cryptic phone call from the Gupta guy, Will and Kevin were both sent home early, and Lou closed up before Monday Night Football even started. Not even the Giants and Pats could bring people out.

The brothers and their employer weren't the only ones feeling the pinch. They'd been born into poverty and, with old businesses and industries shuttered, that was where they'd just have to stay.

There were no upwardly mobile residents in South Side.

It was cold again, and the building's boiler had been acting up all week. The landlord had said he was sending someone to look at it, but unless the guy came after Will went to work at seven in the evening, he hadn't shown. Or maybe he had, and look at it was all he'd done.

The door to the two-bedroom apartment opened and his little sister, Lena, came in with a draft of Arctic air.

"Close the door!" Kevin exclaimed. "It's cold out there."

"I know, dumbass," Lena retorted, slamming the door shut. "I just came in from it. Why aren't you two at work?"

"Lou closed early," Will said, taking his feet off the ottoman so she could get to the couch. "If this cold doesn't break soon, we're in a world of shit."

Lena dropped her backpack on the floor and plopped onto the couch. "I should quit school and get a job."

"No!" the two brothers exclaimed at the same time, both turning to face her.

"It was Mom's dream that you'd get a degree," Will said.

"Yeah, well, it wasn't mine," she said with a scoff. "But that was the only thing the money coulda been used for, so to me, it's a stepping stone to New York."

Their mother had passed away just a year after their father disappeared, but not before getting Lena accepted to college, with her first two years prepaid. Will and Kevin had footed the bill for this year, telling her that Mom had prepaid it, as well.

"We're not homeless," Kevin said. "We'll get by. We always do."

"Not homeless *yet*," Lena said with a scowl. "Who's winning?"

"Tied, three to three," Kevin replied. "Just started a few minutes ago."

Lena turned to Will. "Hey, did that weird guy ever call you back?"

Will shook his head. "Not counting on it. Probably a Nigerian prince."

"Do you believe the stories?" she asked, sitting back and putting her feet up beside his.

"Course not," Kevin said. "Why would our great-granddad desert his family like that?"

"I've been doing some reading on it," Will said. "A bunch of high-ranking German officers escaped to South America, and some of them got out with a lot of money."

"Ha!" Kevin exclaimed. "First down! He wasn't a high-ranking officer. Besides, what good would German money be in South America?"

"Some had art collections that were stolen from museums," Will said. "Loot from local banks sometimes ended up in some general's safe, and when they fled Germany, they apparently liquidated everything in Switzerland for gold. You can use that anywhere. Some escaped with up to a hundred pounds of pure gold, worth fifty thousand U.S. dollars at the time."

Lena looked at him quizzically. "That's what the guy said Dad was after, right? Gold?"

"Fifty grand won't get you far," Kevin said.

"A hundred pounds of gold *today*," Will began, "would be worth about six *million*."

"*Dollars?*" Kevin exclaimed.

"I know what I'd be willing do to lay my hands on it," Lena said.

Will glanced at his sister. She'd said more than once that if it took sleeping with or killing every Wall Street executive she met, she'd do it.

"I'm afraid to ask," Will said.

"I'd slit a fucker's throat in a second," she replied, stone-faced.

Will didn't like hearing his little sister talk rough. She was only twenty-one, and had the looks of a top model, tall and slender, with big blue eyes and long, naturally blond hair. But she had a mean streak that was as wide as she was beautiful.

She did have a point, though. All three of them had done things in the last few years, just to get by, that they wouldn't normally do. Petty theft, moving some weed, or hustling out-of-towners down on Highland Street. Lena had even slept with one of her teachers for $300. She'd said he was hot and would have done it for free anyway.

Something else he didn't like about his sister.

Will's phone trilled like a cricket, and Lena jumped.

"Do you gotta have bug sounds for your ringtone?" she complained.

When Will looked at the screen, it was blank.

"It's him!" he whisper-shouted, sitting up. "The Hadji guy who said he knew Dad."

"Answer it," Kevin said, muting the TV as the Patriots lined up for a forty-four-yard field goal.

"I'll put him on speaker and tell him you're listening." Will touched the screen twice, then laid the phone on the ottoman. "Hello?"

"You are with Kevin and Lena?" the same voice as before asked.

"Yes," Will replied, puzzled he seemed to know that. "And you're on speaker."

"Very good, Wilem. That will save me—"

"Don't call me that," he said. "It's Will. Will Crittenden."

"My apologies," the man said. "And for your brother and sister, my name is Manish Gupta."

"Hi," they both said in unison. Kevin even waved.

"I was a friend of your father and his brother," Gupta said. "I was helping them—"

"Yeah, yeah," Will said. "I already told them all that. Now you tell me something."

"I would be most happy to."

Will leaned toward the phone. "How do you know our names, and that Kevin and Lena were here with me?"

"Because I am in a car parked just outside your apartment building," Gupta replied. "I am afraid the timetable has been moved up. The gold was moved earlier today."

CHAPTER THIRTEEN

At 0900, we arrived at the Coast Guard station at Trumbo Point, Key West, and I could see the America SubDive ship tied up at the long pier.

America had a dark, greenish-gray hull and a gleaming white superstructure. It was massive; at least 140 feet long, with a bow that rose a good twenty feet above the water's surface, giving it the look of an ice breaker.

The roof of the raised pilothouse was ten feet above the bow and had rails around the top, maybe to serve as an observation platform, but I couldn't see any flybridge controls up there. Within the rails were the radar domes, masts, and antennas, plus air intakes and dry exhaust stacks port and starboard.

The work deck was low and extended more than half the length of the ship. Scuppers showed the deck height just a few feet above the water, but the solid bulwarks looked integral to the hull, rising several feet above the deck to minimize the amount of water a large wave hitting broadside might produce, as well as preventing anyone being swept overboard between lifelines.

Overall, she looked very sturdy and capable of going out in almost any sea conditions.

At the stern was a double-armed hydraulic gantry crane for launching and retrieving the submersibles. It had a crossmember between the two arms and spanned the full width of the slightly rounded transom.

Either arm looked much bigger than the davit on *Taranis's* aft flybridge, so I figured the double gantry on *America* was probably capable of a lot more than Stuart and his crew were using it for.

She screamed of overkill; a 150-foot ship to launch and retrieve a pair of ten-foot-long submersibles? It took the meaning of "go big or go home" to a whole new level....

But I figured for a commercial deep dive operation, they needed to be able to work in just about any kind of weather and sea state, *and* stay on site for long periods.

"Wow!" Alberto exclaimed, climbing out of *The Beast* and looking across the water at the ship. "Is that it?"

I pointed to the stern. "There's *Voyager* and *Nomad*."

The two submersibles were on either side of the work deck, close to the stern. They looked to be nearly as wide as they were long, maybe eight by ten feet, and probably six feet in height.

As we started around to the pier, I saw Stuart approaching and waving a hand.

"You're right on time," he called out.

When we met at the foot of the pier, I introduced him to Rusty, Larry, Savannah, and Alberto.

He shook hands with each, then turned to me. "When you said you were bringin' your son, I was thinkin' he'd be in his twenties or thirties."

"I'm adopted," Alberto said, straight-faced.

He liked to see people's reactions to the obvious difference in age, not to mention race.

Stu looked at him for a moment, then grinned. "I was thinkin' you were the result of his marryin' this much younger woman."

Alberto laughed and Savannah smiled.

"Jesse *is* older," she said. "But not by much. Our three girls are a good bit older than Alberto."

Stu turned to face me. He looked the same, but older than I remembered. When I'd retired, he'd been a twenty-four-year-old sergeant. He was still built like a gymnast and probably didn't have an ounce of fat on his 150-pound frame.

"You haven't changed a bit," Stu said. "Still the biggest, ugliest, Marine I ever met."

I chuckled and extended my hand. "And you still look like Baryshnikov."

He grabbed my hand and pumped it. "Damn, it's good to see you again!"

Then he turned to Rusty. "When did you serve, devil dog?"

"Seventy-nine to eighty-three," Rusty said. "Infantry."

"Get some!" Stu snapped, shaking Rusty's hand again. "Ninety-three to seventeen, also infantry."

"Ooh-rah!" Rusty grunted.

Stu turned toward me. "So what's your interest in submersibles?"

"I've been certified," I replied. "Unlimited Master's license, too. I made a couple of shallow dives when I captained a research vessel."

"You? Captained?"

"We lived on *Ambrosia* for two years," Alberto said.

"*Ambro*—" He paused and looked at me. "For real?"

It wasn't surprising that Stuart knew of Armstrong Research and *Ambrosia*. I'm sure they'd crossed wakes at some point.

"Before Jack asked me to captain *Ambrosia*," I explained, "I provided occasional transport for them on my charter boat."

"Well, come on then," Stu said, turning and motioning us to follow him. "I met Jack Armstrong a couple of times. Solid as they come. Did you know that crusty Airborne colonel who was his head of security?"

"Travis Stockwell?" Savannah asked. "Yes, he was part of our crew and still runs Jack's security."

Stu glanced over at me and grinned. "You were captain?" he asked rhetorically. "And he was part of the crew?"

I grinned back at him. "Mostly *outside* my chain of command."

"I'd like to have been there the times he wasn't," Stu said, approaching the boarding gate. "Please, step aboard."

"How big is she?" Rusty asked.

"*America* displaces a little bit over one thousand tons," Stu replied. "That's fully loaded and tanked up for two months at sea. Her overall length is 150 feet, with a thirty-six-foot beam, and a draft of ten."

"Way bigger than *Taranis*," Alberto said.

"That's our trimaran," Savannah explained. "Almost as wide, but only sixty-six feet long."

"Are the amas just for balance?" he asked. "Or living quarters?"

"Two staterooms in the port ama," she replied. "And the master head in the other."

He cocked an eyebrow. "Just the head?"

"The master stateroom is a third of the main deck," I told him. "It and the salon are nearly full beam with wide side decks."

"That sounds roomy," Stu said, following us down the ramp to the work deck, just aft of midships. "We have about that in working deck space here, but quarters are a bit cramped. Up to twenty people in six cabins."

"And all the accommodations are in the forward part?" Savannah asked.

"Yes, ma'am," he replied. "Below the work deck is the engine and mechanical room."

"That's gotta be a sight," Rusty said, surveying the work deck.

"We'll go down there later if you like."

"Oh, he'll like," I said with a chuckle. "Rusty's a gearhead."

Larry and Alberto had walked out onto the massive work deck, looking at all the equipment but heading toward the submersibles.

"Twin diesels," Rusty said, noting the dry stacks high above. "With a closed loop coolin' system, and I'm guessin' two big diesel gen-sets?"

"Plus another diesel forward," Stu replied. "A 360-horsepower bow thruster."

"Whoa!" Rusty exclaimed. "That'll turn her around. What're the main engines?"

"Twin Cummins," Stu replied. "Rated at 850-horsepower continuous output."

"Check it out, Dad!" Alberto called from the stern. "It's like the *Popemobile*!"

CHAPTER FOURTEEN

The submersibles sat on cradles on either side of the stern, and the gantry overhead had a hoist that could be traversed from one side to the other to launch or retrieve either one quickly and efficiently. There were identical workbenches and cabinets on both sides of each submersible, which I assumed held tools and parts for inspecting and repairing each one.

The enclosures looked like clear acrylic bubbles with the bottoms half-wrapped by a metal superstructure connecting two long ballast tanks on either side.

The upper half of the bubble *did* look like the roof of the car the Pope rode in. Or the Jetson's flying car, maybe. But Alberto would have no idea about that.

"Each one has four thrusters," Stu explained. "Two in the stern for horizontal propulsion forward and backward, and two up front to raise and lower the bow."

I looked inside. "Joystick?"

He nodded. "They also have four hydroplanes for maneuvering, two forward and two aft, and the ballast tanks are synced with a high pressure air pump. The stick controls all the thrusters, planes, and air ballast, so it will bank when turning, like a ray would."

If I had to guess, they could probably turn completely around within their own length, and move up or down in varying degrees of pitch or roll. The exterior was studded with quite a few lights, pointing in all directions.

Inside, each had side-by-side seating for two occupants, with a single joystick control and instrument panel in the center.

"It's set up differently than I imagined," Savannah said. "I thought you'd have to lie down in it."

I gave her a wicked grin, knowing exactly what she was thinking. A romantic dive on a reef. Or at least I hoped so.

"Each of our Triton 1000/2 submersibles can carry two pilots to a maximum depth of one thousand feet," Stu said, continuing around *Voyager*. "Both are untethered submersibles and operate on internal battery power, which, under normal dive operations, gives us about ten hours of underwater exploration or inspection."

"How long would the air last?" Savannah asked.

"Once sealed up, internal scrubbers clean the air of excess carbon dioxide, much like a diver's closed-circuit rebreather system would. Downside—the scrubbers have to be replaced every fifty hours of operation. We err on the safe side and replace them every forty. And they're expensive."

"But no decompression limits," Larry said. "That's a big plus."

"Because we remain at one atmosphere of pressure inside the sub, there aren't any limits for the divers." He shrugged. "Except maybe boredom. Basically, you can stay down as long as the batteries last. With a reserve to get back to the surface, that is."

"We'll probably go with a tethered one," I said. "It's what *Taranis* is set up for."

"We do a lot of oil rig inspections," Stu said. "A thousand-foot umbilical could be too easy to get tangled. Most tethered submersibles will be like you thought, one or two people, lying prone inside a steel tube with portholes."

Savannah returned my wicked smile.

"*Voyager* is as basic as they come," Stu said. "Essentially, an underwater viewing platform. But *Nomad* is equipped with robotic arms for moving or grabbing things."

"Like a treasure chest," Rusty said.

"We've been hired to do a few deep treasure dives," Stu replied. "In most cases, the treasure hunter came out on the short end."

Stuart continued to show us around the work deck, and we were even allowed to get inside the submersibles. At six-three and two-twenty, the seat was a pretty tight fit for me, but the actual interior was definitely roomier than the one we'd had on *Ambrosia*.

Besides the subs and their workstations, there was a thirty-foot cargo container on one side of the work deck that was set up for open water scuba diving, complete with air compressors, tanks, buoyancy compensators, and all sorts of commercial and technical dive gear.

It looked like enough to outfit a team of six, and Stuart explained that their recovery crew was usually a three-man team, so they could rotate if they needed to or double deploy to retrieve both submersibles at once.

"Besides conducting recoveries," Stu explained, "our dive teams also perform the shallower parts of the inspections, down to sixty feet. We even have a hyperbaric chamber on the work deck."

The tour continued below deck in the engine room, and it was equally impressive, with standing headroom in a huge open bay that had two rows of steel support posts down the middle.

Besides the two main engines and generators, there was a large reverse osmosis unit and several water chillers for air conditioning systems. Assorted pumps were mounted on easily accessed stands with all piping running together, both horizontally and vertically, and each one marked every four feet or so.

There was room to walk around every piece of equipment for servicing and you could eat off the deck.

Stu knew the boat inside and out, every spec, every system, and every piece of hardware and software. The ship could make enough electricity and water to supply a small village almost indefinitely.

"Want to go up to the bridge for a bit?" Stu asked, looking at his watch. "Lunch'll be on in about thirty minutes or so. The rest of the crew should start to crawl out about then."

I checked my own watch. It was 1030 and my stomach was starting to rumble.

"Sounds good to me," I said. "Just out of curiosity, what does one of those untethered submersibles run?"

"A little over two-and-a-half mil," Stu said. "Brand new. But that's just the starting price, and the 1000/2 series is about the lowest-priced submersible Triton offers."

"Where's all the crew?" Alberto asked.

"Still asleep," Stu replied. "As we got close to Key West last night, we had all hands on watch but two. This is one of the busiest places I know of, so far as boat traffic goes. I took over the watch when we docked, along with one other guy. He went into town to provision as soon as we were cleared into the country."

The bridge deck was as organized and spotless as the rest of the ship, with a well laid-out instrument panel at the helm, a navigation station to port, and a communications center to starboard. Hatches opened to the side decks on both sides, and there was a watch berth aft.

Alberto went straight to the sonar controls. "This is the same as we had on *Ambrosia*."

"Almost the same," Stu said. "Our sonar system includes a

communications transducer to talk to the submersibles up to half a mile away. We also use extremely low frequency radio signals."

"How low?" Larry asked. "I thought radio didn't work underwater."

"In the three- to three-hundred-hertz range," Stu replied. "It's good to about three hundred meters, making it a much more secure means of communication than acoustics."

With his electrical engineering degree background, Larry jumped into a technical conversation that even I could only pick up on a little.

We ended the tour on the mess deck, where several crew members were already eating and drinking coffee. It was set up cafeteria-style, with a chalkboard menu hanging on the wall. The guy behind the counter was pleasant and took our orders efficiently.

When it was my turn, I glanced over at the menu board, and right there at the top was a blackened mahi sandwich.

CHAPTER FIFTEEN

We said our goodbyes shortly after lunch, and I ducked my head in the galley to thank the chef. The only one there was the guy who took our orders.

"Did you make that mahi sandwich?" I asked him.

He smiled and nodded.

"One of the best I've ever had," I told him. "And it's my go-to order wherever I find it."

"Stu said you were a charter skipper," the man said with an Australian accent as he extended a hand. "Name's Nigel Kincaid, from Western Australia."

"Pleased to meet you," I said, shaking his hand. "Jesse McDermitt, from up island."

"This whole crew bloody well knows who you are, mate," Nigel said, his smile genuine. "Even if ol' Stu didn't serve with ya and talk about ya."

"How so?" I asked.

"Fair dinkum?" he replied. "Every bloke on this tub is a treasure hunter in one way or other, mate."

"Yeah, well, it was a great blackened mahi," I said, snapping a two-finger salute.

"If you ever need a cook on an expedition," he said, "you know where to find me."

As I joined the others at the boarding ramp, Stu was promising to come down from Lauderdale one Saturday for Rusty's lionfish cookout. Then we all piled back into *The Beast* for the hour-long drive up island.

As I drove through town, the talk was more about the submersibles and the ship itself. But in my mind, the ship was the prize. I could see *America* making the Northern Passage or Cape Horn to Antarctica.

"Given the option," Rusty said as we made the last turn and started across the short bridge to Stock Island, "I'd go for one of those untethered ones. Especially for pokin' around old wrecks and such."

"But is it worth a million more?" I asked. "It's not like we have a lot of 'poking around' time left."

"Do I get a vote?" Alberto chimed in.

When we finished laughing, I looked in the mirror at him. "Do you have a million bucks in chess winnings you're not telling us about?"

He crossed his arms. "A tether could be a problem around a shallow reef. The wind could change and move the boat, and that would drag the tether across live coral. They're more for unobstructed vertical dives."

"Where'd you learn that?" I asked, glancing again in the mirror.

I hadn't thought of the damage a long cord could do to the reef, and the danger that would cause, even in a shallow dive.

"From a bunch of places," he replied. "You also gotta look at run time and maintenance for the generator and compressor."

"I have to agree," Savannah said. "For what you plan to use it for, whether that's diving a wall, sitting beside a reef, or finding things lost to the sea, untethered would be better and safer."

"I used ChatGPT," Alberto said, "and guess what? There's a two-year wait to rent one."

Two thoughts besides the higher price sticker popped quickly into my mind. First, I realized I'd wasted a lot of time and money setting *Taranis* up for the same kind of submersible operation we'd had on *Ambrosia*, and second, how much room a sub like the two we'd looked at would take up on the flybridge deck. It was designed for a lot smaller. The weight wasn't a concern—the cradle was just off center of the main hull. But the larger footprint would mean losing deck or lounge space.

Just then, my phone vibrated in my pocket and the Bluetooth display on the dash told me Billy was calling. I tapped *Accept* on the touchscreen and said, "Hey, Billy. We're heading back up island from Key West. You're on speaker."

"Who is with you?" he asked, sounding as if he were at the bottom of a deep well.

"Savvy, Alberto, Rusty, and Larry, my new caretaker."

There was a short pause.

"You and Rusty need to come here right away," he finally said, an edge to his voice.

"Come where?" I asked. "What's going on?"

"I came down to Whitewater Bay early this morning… you both just need to come here."

I fished my phone out, slowing as we got to a passing zone, then disconnected the Bluetooth, and held the phone to my ear. "You're off speaker," I said. "Talk to me."

"I brought tools with me, including a grinder," he said. "I've been wondering about those welded torpedo tubes, so I cut the welds and opened them. They're full of gold, Jesse."

"What?" I shouted.

"Swiss-stamped, 400-troy-ounce, solid gold bars," Billy replied, his voice a little shaky. "A lot of them. They're stacked in there like bricks, and each one weighs at least twenty pounds."

"Over twenty-five," I breathed, as I glanced in the mirror and saw the concern in Rusty's expression. "We'll be there before sunset. Did you fly or take your blow boat?"

"The airboat," he replied. "I sent the FCW people home when I got here, but their relief will arrive at six."

I glanced at the clock on the dash as the last of the impatient drivers went around us at the end of the passing zone. It was a little after 1300.

"We'll be wheels up in ninety minutes," I told Billy. "And be where you are by 1600 at the latest. Do we need to bring anything?"

"Strong backs," he replied.

I ended the call and thought about pulling over. This was huge and I was suddenly nervous. A single 400-ounce gold bar was worth well over a million dollars—I wasn't real sure what the current price was; I hadn't checked it in probably a year or more. And two dozen of them would be eight figures. Close to thirty million.

"What's wrong?" Rusty asked. "Is the sub okay?"

I looked back at him again. "Yeah, the sub's fine," I replied. "Billy got the torpedo tubes open."

"Oh no," Savannah said. "Don't tell me there were live torpedoes in them."

I glanced over at her and shook my head, then looked back at Rusty and Larry again.

"Larry, I need you to keep this to yourself," I said, then locked eyes with Rusty. "Billy said the tubes are filled with gold bars."

CHAPTER SIXTEEN

After I explained what Billy had told me, Rusty jumped into action immediately, getting on his phone with one person after another, as the rest of us digested what lay ahead.

"I don't need to tell you how important it is that this information doesn't get out," I said, glancing at Larry in the mirror. "We have to keep this thing under wraps until we know what we're dealing with. Billy doesn't know you, but I do, and I know you will."

"You can count on it," Larry replied.

Finally, Rusty called Billy back. "I got ya on speaker, bro. Jesse's friend here is good to go; we can talk openly."

"You and Jesse need to get—"

"We're coming as fast as we can," I said over my shoulder. "We need a plan. Larry lives with us on the island. I trust him as I do you, brother."

"We're not keepin' this gold, Billy," Rusty said. "We all agree, and I know you will too, that the bulk of it needs to be returned to its legal or cultural owners if possible."

There was a lengthy pause, then Billy sighed. "It is good to hear you say that."

"Do you know how many bars we're talkin'?" Rusty asked.

"Twenty-four," Billy whispered.

"That's over thirty million dollars!" Alberto exclaimed.

"Let's call it thirty *even*," Rusty said. "We reimburse our recovery expenses up to today, takin' that right off the top, then a ten percent salvor's fee that we'll split three ways and donate the rest to the right people."

"Is that ethical?" Savannah asked.

"Every bit as much as salvagin' the sub," Rusty said. "Even more so. Some salvors charge fifty percent. But we ain't gotta be greedy."

"We're coming into Big Pine now, Billy," I said. "Savvy called ahead and *Island Hopper's* all gassed up and ready. We should be there by 1500. What do you want to do? It's your find and Rusty's the salvor. I'm just an investor."

"Get it off the sub," he replied without pause. "And stored somewhere safe until we figure out who to return it to."

"Jesse's island," Rusty stated. "Safest place I know."

I glanced in the mirror. "I think Billy meant like putting it in a vault at a bank."

"No, Rusty's right," Billy said. "Moving something like this in public and putting it in a local Keys bank... word's bound to get out."

"How much will it weigh?" Larry asked.

"Over eight hundred pounds," Alberto answered, again looking at his phone. "Eight-thirteen."

"Your Beaver can carry that easily," Billy said. "Even with the two of you in it."

I caught Larry's expression in the mirror as he looked out at the mangroves flashing past. He was thinking adventure.

"You said bring a strong back," I said. "Larry's coming with us."

"I'll clear it with Lauren," Larry said, trying to get his phone out of his pocket with his lap belt on.

"Okay," Rusty said. "We're all agreed. I got some other calls to make. Herman's already workin' on the crew manifest. It's prolly safe to say that *Seaman* Johan Schmidt was actually Colonel or General Johan Schmidt, but Herman's pretty certain the captain woulda used real names."

"Why does that matter?" Alberto asked.

"That's where we start looking for rightful heirs," Rusty said. "We look wherever these particular Nazis looted. They kept records and Herman's gonna start working on a probable list."

"Just get here before the water cops get back," Billy said. "They make me nervous enough without all this shiny stuff lying around."

Rusty ended the call as we started out onto the Seven Mile Bridge and he leaned forward. "This'll be the easiest recovery I ever brokered, and I feel kinda guilty for takin' that little bit. But it'll fly through, smooth as butter. And it *does* solve an imminent problem for you, bro."

"What's that?" I asked looking up at the mirror.

"A third of ten percent is a cool million bucks each to me, you, and Billy," he replied, grinning. "Right there's *your* sub. We should take 'em for a dive together."

Savannah covered her mouth, stifling a laugh. "He was going to get it anyway."

I looked over and nodded. "Remember that night wall dive in Belize the first time we were there?"

"The first time?" Alberto asked. "You went before we did last year?"

"Several years ago," Savannah said, turning to face him. "Flo was just a teenager. We sailed down on *Salty Dog*, and I remember the water was much clearer then than it was last summer."

Salty Dog was a Formosa ketch I'd donated to the Alex DuBois McDermitt Flyfishing School for troubled teens on Grassy Key. It was named for my late second wife, an accomplished angler from the Pacific Northwest. She'd been murdered on our wedding night.

"I remember you didn't want to return to the surface," I said, glancing over at Savannah again. "I almost had to *drag* you out of that little cave. What if we could stay there the whole night?"

Savannah looked over and smiled.

"What time of year was it?" Alberto asked. "When you went the first time."

"It was in the spring, wasn't it?" Savannah asked, looking over at me.

"April of 2020." I replied. "Covid lockdown at sea."

"Whoa… really?" Alberto asked.

"Yes," Savannah replied. "We spent a good bit of that spring and summer out in the Ragged Islands, and Jack Armstrong had supplies dropped every couple of weeks for us and a few other liveaboards who got stranded beyond borders. Even America wouldn't have let us back in."

"We *could* have returned," I corrected, looking over and grinning at Savannah beside me. "After we'd been isolated there four weeks, we could have cleared in pretty easy. But we really liked it there."

"Okay, that's what I thought," Rusty said, raising his voice as he ended a whispered phone conversation. "I'll get back to ya this evenin'."

"Who was that?" I asked over my shoulder, as we entered Marathon. "And why all the hush-hush, secret-squirrel stuff?"

"Just gettin' the right permits set up," he replied. "And makin' sure I know the right palms to grease."

CHAPTER SEVENTEEN

Instead of going back to the Rusty Anchor, we headed straight for the airport, where I pulled around to my hangar and parked with the engine running. Savannah and Alberto were going to take *The Beast* back to Rusty's place to get the Grady and return to the island. Then we'd meet them there after picking up the gold.

Rusty and I climbed into *Island Hopper's* cockpit as Larry got in back, and then I went through the startup and preflight checklists, making sure everything was working as it should and we were topped up with fuel. Then I "walked" the big radial engine through two revolutions, bumping the starter for a third of a turn at a time with the magnetos turned off to allow any oil that had accumulated in the lower cylinders to drain into the exhaust manifolds.

When I cranked the engine again with the magnetos on, it stumbled once, caught, belched blue-gray smoke, then began running a little rough before quickly leveling out at a smooth, loping idle, the sound of raw power.

I announced my intention on the unicom frequency and taxied to the west end of the runway. I made a second announcement, and not hearing a reply, pulled onto the runway.

In minutes, we were in the air and headed north toward Whitewater Bay, the Nazi sub, and a treasure in gold that we were certain came from the looting of wealthy businesses, individuals, towns, banks, and local governments by the Nazis during World War II. And now, all we had to do was to figure out where the bulk of the riches came from.

A monumental task for sure.

I banked north and climbed slowly into a clear blue sky, the sun already halfway to the western horizon.

"Anything new from Herman?" I asked Rusty, who was scrolling through his phone.

"Matter of fact, he thinks he was spot on with the names," Rusty said. "Germans were always big sticklers for details, and the crew manifest we found in the captain's logbook wasn't the crew that left Germany and was reported lost at sea. Almost every crewman's name on the one we found matches the names of a half-dozen regular army generals, two Gestapo colonels, and one admiral."

"Bingo," Larry said from the back seat. "I know an AI app that can cross-reference those names to where the units they commanded occupied Europe against known thefts from those occupied territories."

Rusty turned in his seat and looked back at Larry. "Do what?"

"Artificial intelligence," Larry replied. "It's great for just this kind of research, not to mention engineering problems."

"You mean a computer? I got one of those."

Larry laughed. "Think of it as a computer connected to every other computer in the world, and you have the internet. Then let the computer learn everything there is to know from the internet. It can answer complex questions, given specific parameters. It'll match names to locations, then determine the value of any thefts in those areas and the probability of who stole what."

"Ask it what?" I asked, looking in the mirror as I leveled off at twenty-five-hundred feet. "Hey computer, where did these guys steal from?"

Larry shook his head. "Broad questions yield broad answers. You'd have to be more specific. Give it the names of the officers and ask it to research the campaigns they commanded, and what treasures were likely stolen from those areas. Things like that. Then give it the amount of money gained in 1945 Swiss francs, and ask it where the money likely came from. That'd be a start, and you could refine the questions from there. It'll cross-check all known facts and give a probable prediction of what was looted from where that roughly equals the gold's value at the time."

"Artificial *intelligence*, huh?" Rusty said. "Ain't that what that movie, *Terminator,* was all about?"

"Do you think that's what Herman's using?" I asked, glancing over at Rusty.

"He's an engineer," Rusty said. "Who knows?"

We flew in silence for a few minutes, the blue waters of the Gulf of Mexico stretching away to the horizon in all directions.

Finally, I turned to Rusty. "What are you thinking of doing with your share? If this goes through."

"Oh, it'll sure enough go through," Rusty said. "Ain't no doubt about that. Who's gonna turn down thirty mil?"

He was silent for a moment, staring through the windshield in thought. "Jules and the boys are all set," he said softly. "Maybe it's time for me and Sid to retire."

"Retire?" I asked in surprise. "You've tended that bar for the better part of fifty years. What else are you going to do?"

"Sid wants to travel," he replied. "See Ireland, where her people come from. Maybe swing up through Norway from there."

"Is that where your family's from?" Larry asked him. "Thurman is Scandinavian, right?"

"I know every Thurman in an unbroken line," Rusty said proudly, "all the way back to the eleventh century in what's now Norway."

"Did you ever contact that guy on Ancestry?" I asked, his comment reminding me. "Your brother-cousin?"

"He ain't no brother," Rusty said. "If someone was related in more than one branch of the tree, I reckon that might look like a first cousin, at least percentage-wise."

"Jerry! Jerry!" I chanted.

He punched my shoulder. "I messaged the guy through the app," he replied. "I'm still thinkin' it's a screwup somehow."

"I hear those things are pretty accurate," Larry said. "Like one in a billion chance."

"*I'd* like to see some of the world, too," Rusty said, switching the topic back. "Except for the time I was in the Corps, I hardly ever been outta the Keys, 'cept a handful of times. Mom and Pop did it, and they went to six of seven continents, too; several dozen countries. And they weren't much younger than me and Sid are now."

Rusty's father had sold the place to me and Rusty when we were in our first year in the Corps. I only went in on it because Rusty couldn't afford to without a bank loan. Rusty's dad, Shorty Thurman, had been offered good money by a developer, who would probably have bulldozed the place and put up condos. Shorty agreed to stay on until Rusty got out of the Corps, and then he and Dreama went off to the South Pacific for their first destination.

"Then you should do it," I said to Rusty. "Take Sidney and see the world. What'll you do with the Anchor?"

"Give it to Jules, I reckon."

I laughed. "Yeah, I can totally see Deuce as a bartender."

"He likes doin' it," Rusty said. "You know, when he and Julie bring the boys down every other weekend, Deuce emails me a list of things I need done, so I can be the bad guy and make 'em work."

I laughed again. "I've seen you working with Trey and Jim. They enjoy helping you and you love doing it with them. You and Deuce are both good role models for a strong work ethic."

"Yeah, well, it's gettin' harder to keep up with 'em."

I chuckled. "Boys do tend to get stronger with age."

"And grandpas get weaker," he groused. "That ain't right."

CHAPTER EIGHTEEN

Manish Gupta waited patiently by a public boat ramp in North Miami. It was midafternoon, and no sign of his contact yet. Of course, he'd arrived early and the appointed time wasn't for another five minutes, but he was anxious.

He'd used his computer skills to locate the salvage operator, then his cell phone, which he could track. Over the course of the last several months, he'd noticed it in the same remote part of the Everglades where his two patsies had been when they'd disappeared. Over time, he'd located two other cell phones in close proximity to the salvors, at the same time he was in that area, and recently he'd discovered another wireless device, but it wasn't a phone.

Yesterday, all four devices were in that same location, which Manish was certain was the location of the submarine. The newest device had been very active, moving all around the salvor's device, along with one of the other cell phones he'd been tracking.

He'd checked the locations all through the day, and two had moved at a very high speed to a spot sixteen kilometers from the others. But then the others had slowly moved toward it, throughout the day.

He'd decided the new device was actually a Wi-Fi enabled camera, and had spent nearly an hour trying to hack it. He'd finally retrieved a still photograph, clearly showing what appeared to be the submarine.

And it had been moving, pushed along by a tugboat.

That was a major problem. If they were able to move the submarine to a more populated area, he'd have no way of sending anyone in to retrieve the gold.

Manish preferred virtual meetings whenever possible. Or better still no meeting at all. He'd rather just send the information and wait for the results.

The L-shaped dock by the ramp was empty, as were the ramps themselves, and more than half the parking lot. Big pickup trucks with boat trailers filled many of the spots. It being a Tuesday, he decided they were probably owned by people who worked on the water. He considered it unlikely that many of the rigs were owned by pleasure boaters. But he didn't like boats, so what did he know?

He'd been working on this project for a very long time, picking up tidbits of information here, unsubstantiated rumors and stories there, then organizing the information and getting others to do the heavy lifting.

At first he'd recruited the grandsons and granddaughter of the submarine's captain, knowing that they would be intrigued. But Karl Crittenden, his brother, Lucas, and their cousins, Paul Schmidt and Hanna Hoffman had all disappeared without a trace.

Manish felt certain that they'd gone rogue and tried to go after the treasure themselves. In which case, based on recently discovered information, they had likely been dispatched very quickly.

After much research, he'd learned the identity of two of the three cell phone owners who frequented the location. The first had been fairly easy. The salvage operator lived in Marathon, down in the Keys, and owned a restaurant called the Rusty

Anchor. His name was James Thurman. The second one had been more difficult, but after months of tracking, he'd noticed the phone was in two places, forty miles apart, every Friday afternoon. One was a convalescent home for old people, and the second was the headquarters of the Seminole Nation. That location was visited at exactly the same time every week, and stayed for two hours.

A lot of cross-checking of the leaders of the Seminole finally revealed that one person who was on the council had had someone living in the home, a very old man named William Rainwater, Sr.

That led him to the son, William Jr., and after a lot more research he learned that he and the salvor had both been in the Marines at the same time and stationed in some of the same places.

The brothers and cousins had gone up against two ex-Marines and paid the ultimate price for their mistake.

After that loss, Manish had been forced to give up, knowing that whoever had found it had likely found the gold. But just recently, new information had rekindled his hope that at least the gold hadn't been found yet.

The discovery of the U-320 had been made public just a few weeks earlier, with no mention of the vast wealth it surely must have contained, and the location proved to be where the captain's grandsons had predicted, and where they'd died.

Apparently, a series of navigation errors and a hurricane had conspired to drive the submarine deep into the Everglades in South Florida, where it had sat unnoticed for eight decades.

Manish couldn't imagine a place so remote being just a hundred or so kilometers from the glitzy metropolis surrounding him.

Recently, the bar owner and part-time salvor in the Keys had discovered the submarine, declaring it a derelict vessel, and had then gotten the rights to salvage it.

Of course, Manish knew that the salvor, or someone else, had discovered the wreck years ago. And that someone was probably responsible for the missing descendants of the submarine's original and only captain, Hans Crittenden, Sr. who was then a *leutnant zur see* or navy sub-lieutenant, the lowest officer rank in the German navy.

Every passenger the good *leutnant* had carried aboard his ship was at the extreme other end of the rank structure: colonels, generals, and admirals, all with vast wealth stolen from the Jewish people of Amsterdam during the occupation. The accumulated wealth had been sold and turned into gold.

At first, Manish had assumed the salvage operation would have been running a barge out to the location to start cutting the submarine up for scrap metal. No matter where the gold had been hidden, the salvors would likely have found it during the dismantling.

So why the long wait? Manish thought, looking out over the water at a boat coming in. Why didn't the salvor begin right away? Had they first stripped anything of value?

A week ago, Manish had learned that a series of canals and even a lock were being built to *move* the submarine out of the Everglades, completely intact.

And now he'd seen it first-hand. A recent photograph, obviously shot from an airplane, was sent from William Rainwater, Jr.'s wireless camera to James Thurman's cell phone.

But who was the fourth man? he wondered.

Whoever he was, he rarely sent text messages on his phone, spent a lot of his time on an island in the Keys that could only be reached by boat, and knew somebody who owned an airplane, or perhaps had one himself. Whenever he made a voice call from his phone, it rarely lasted more than a few seconds, and intercepting live phone calls took a moment. At most, he'd heard the man say goodbye a half dozen times.

The approaching boat turned toward the day dock where Manish stood, feeling very out of place.

The boat had two men on it, both older and probably retired. They tied their boat to the dock efficiently, then one got out and walked past Manish, heading to the parking lot.

So, he moved a little farther toward the end of the L-shaped dock.

Using the vast resources of the consortium he worked for, Manish had learned that the planned canal was mostly finished before the discovery was announced, and at present, only needed the lock built and a short dredging of a nearby creek before the submarine could be moved into open water. Construction on that wouldn't start for another month.

The question was, had they found the gold yet?

For now, he'd hold that information close. He knew a large amount of gold had been moved onto the submarine in 1944, and the submarine had now been discovered. That's what he'd been paid to find out, and what he would tell his new contact.

Another boat approached, also with two men aboard. It angled toward the end of the dock, both men eyeing him warily and checking the parking lot, the green area beyond it, and the water all around.

The boat idled toward Manish, and one of the men went to the front to keep it from colliding with the dock.

"Are you Gupta?" the man in front asked.

Manish nodded. This was the worst part of his job. He didn't have a problem sending men after a target, often at great risk to themselves, but he just didn't like meeting with them. Or people in general.

"Get in," the man said. "We'll bring you back here after we talk."

He pulled the side of the boat closer, and Manish clumsily stepped down into it.

"I have never been on a boat," he confessed, holding tightly to a rail.

"Just have a seat," the man said, pushing the front of the boat away from the dock. "And move with at least one hand on something that doesn't move."

Manish almost fell into a seat, catching the edge with both hands, then moving around until he could drop onto one of the seats in the front.

The man driving put the engine in gear and idled forward, away from the dock. Then he turned and accelerated slightly, heading back toward the large bay.

The man in front sat down across from Manish, quietly studying his features.

As the boat motored farther away from the shore, the distance raised Manish's anxiety level.

The man across from him was tall and broad-shouldered, with a dark tan, narrow blue eyes, and light-colored hair, cut short. He had a jagged, whitish scar about five centimeters long that ran along the left side of his face, just missing the eye. Manish judged him to be in his early to mid-thirties.

"Why do I want to work with you?" the man finally asked.

"I do not understand," Manish said nervously. "I was told that you would be briefed on the assignment."

"I was," the man said softly. "You're quite the stickler for details, except locations. We'll get to that, but first, why would *I* want to work with *you*?"

"The details I shared are only the basics and overall timetable," Manish said. "However, time is of the essence. I can provide you with ten *million* reasons why you might want to know more. And *only* I can do that."

"And what *are* these ten million reasons?"

"Gold," Manish replied. "I provide logistics along with some viable.... How do you say? Lackeys! I will provide people to take the blame if things go badly. If all works out, you and I will split ten million dollars' worth of gold."

"And who are these fall guys?" the man asked.

"Three siblings," Manish replied. "The sons of the man who had been helping me three years ago, and the great-grandsons of the man who lost the treasure."

"*Treasure*, is it?" the man asked. "Around here, that usually means it's underwater."

"Not necessarily," Manish replied. "At least not now."

"You said three siblings," the man stated. "But only mentioned two great-grandsons. Who's the third?"

"A beautiful young woman," he replied, watching the man's eyes. "The younger sister of the two brothers."

His eyes showed only a moment of a flicker, and then he was back to business. "What's to stop me from just keeping all the gold when we find it?"

He smiled, but Manish saw no humor in his eyes.

"Please do not take me for a fool," he said, mustering what daring he could. "We work for the same people, and they have already invested heavily into this project. I, myself, have been working on this for five years. You and I will be splitting only a *third* of what you recover. You will no more double-cross me than you would the man who sent you here."

"How soon?" the man asked.

"What is your name?"

The man sat up straight, then made a circling motion to the driver with one hand. "My name is Mr. Damien."

"How soon can you move your assets to the southwest coast of Florida?" Manish asked, point-blank. "You will need fast boats and time is quite critical."

"With one call," Mr. Damien replied, "I can have the necessary men and equipment in place before midnight. I just need a precise location for insertion."

Manish nodded. "Then please make the call. The target will be guarded, but it is only two men. The longer it waits, the more likely someone will find the gold."

CHAPTER NINETEEN

I pulled back on the throttle as the southwest coast of Florida started coming into view, then pointed the nose downward slightly as I searched for Whitewater Bay.

As we descended below a thousand feet and I lined up with the whole length of the bay, I called out my intention on the aviation unicom frequency, then did the same on VHF channel sixteen, which most boaters monitored. I knew Billy would have a radio on and I also knew he likely wouldn't answer unless there was a boat in the way or something.

Five minutes later, with the flaps deployed, *Island Hopper* settled onto the water's surface, slowed, and then I turned her toward the U-320, resting near the northeast shore.

With only a few feet of hull and her conning tower out of the water, she was almost invisible against the gray-green backdrop of trees along the bay's eastern shore.

"There's a long dock line in the aft storage compartment of the float on your side," I said to Rusty. "I'll kill the engine and kick the tail around as we get close, and you can throw the line to Billy."

"On it," he said, removing his headset and harness, then opening the hatch.

"Do you need me to do anything?" Larry asked.

I glanced up in the mirror. "Rusty's got it."

When Rusty pushed the hatch open, the roar of the engine got louder, and the propwash buffeted the hatch, pulling at his clothes as he stepped out.

As Rusty got the line ready, I dropped the engine to an idle, then steered us toward the stern of the sub, which was a lot lower than *Island Hopper's* wings, and if I timed it right, Rusty could just hand the line to Billy.

Fifty feet away, I shut off the engine and stepped on the left rudder pedal.

The Wipaire floats had small rudders at the aft ends to help with maneuvering in water, and *Island Hopper* started turning slowly as Billy walked out toward the stern of the sub.

I didn't get quite close enough, but as Billy ducked under the starboard wing, Rusty was able to throw the line across five or six feet of water to him.

A couple of minutes later, Billy had us tied off, and pulled up close to the sub's port side, so Larry and I had to crawl through the cockpit.

"Thanks for coming so quickly," Billy said. "I don't want anyone to learn about this until we know it's safely hidden."

"That's the best thing all around," Rusty said. "Where is it?"

"Stacked on the deck," Billy replied. "Just below the hatch."

He didn't have to say which hatch. There were five altogether, two larger deck hatches forward and aft on either side for loading torpedoes, as well as the one in the conning tower, which was the only one we'd gotten open.

I climbed up to the observation deck, just a few feet above the main deck, and looked down through the hatch as the others crowded around.

The sight of that many gold bars shining in the bright LED lights we'd installed was like nothing I'd ever seen.

"Alberto said that at today's prices," I whispered, "we're looking at thirty-three-million dollars."

"That's *insane*," Larry breathed, then looked up at Billy. "Hi. I'm Larry."

"Billy," my old friend said, extending his hand.

Larry shook it and I said, "Larry and his wife are good people, brother. They teach at the school on Grassy Key."

Billy nodded, needing no more confirmation, then looked down again. "This won't be easy. I had to carry each one from the torpedo room to get them here. Drop one overboard and it's more than a million dollars lost in the muck."

"There's three buckets in the engine room," Rusty suggested as he started down the ladder. "They're stout enough to hold thirty pounds and they've got strong rope handles. We can put one at a time in 'em, and start a chain."

"You can hand the bars up to Billy," I called down to Rusty, as he stood on the deck below us. "He can put them in a bucket and Larry can carry the buckets over to me on the plane, while you two load the next one."

Rusty disappeared aft as Billy stepped down the ladder far enough to be able to reach Rusty and still have his head and shoulders above the deck.

When Rusty returned, he handed up two of the buckets, which Billy set aside, put one of the bars in the third, then handed it up.

"Damn, that's heavy," Rusty said, as Billy took the rope handle and lifted it to the observation deck.

I hefted the bucket. "Twenty-five pounds."

"Here, Billy," Rusty said, passing up the next bar as I turned to carry the first bucket aft, to where *Island Hopper* was tied up.

Larry would do the next twenty-three trips back and forth

across an unpainted and rusty steel deck, carrying literally buckets full of gold, his stride ungainly due to the weight.

With *Island Hopper* on a starboard tie, I had to lift the bucket into the copilot's seat, climb up, then over it, to the aisle behind the cockpit.

The bars were deceptively heavy, slightly smaller in size than a standard red brick but far heavier.

As I unloaded each successive bucket Larry handed up to the seat, and arranged the bars on the plane's aft deck, Larry carried an empty one back and returned a few minutes later with the next load. It took more than half an hour, and once we got the last of the gold stored aboard *Island Hopper*, we stopped to catch our breath.

"That's a lot of gold," Larry said, as Billy returned from his airboat with bottles of water, and passed them around.

"Almost seven hundred pounds," I said, after covering the gold with a small blanket, and started climbing out. On the deck, I turned to Billy. "You want us to stick around until FWC gets here?"

Billy looked at his watch. "They'll be here in a little over an hour. It would probably be best if you weren't here."

"Too late for that," Rusty said, pointing across the inland bay.

An FWC boat was coming out of the creek and climbing up on plane, heading our way.

Then the lights came on.

CHAPTER TWENTY

It would be extremely difficult to explain the gold, since we weren't ready to divulge the find yet. If the water cops knew we were about to fly out of Whitewater Bay with thirty-three-million-dollars-worth of gold, they'd have to file a report. And I knew all too well how lax local law enforcement was in the digital world. Word would get out.

Still, these guys worked for Kim, and I felt bad about the deception.

"Is your blow boat loaded?" Rusty asked Billy. "With all the tools ya brought?"

Billy looked forward to where his airboat was tied alongside the conning tower. "No, they are still down in the torpedo room."

"Ya gonna need 'em for the next week?"

Billy shook his head. "No."

Rusty turned to me. "You still got those flexible solar panels on your plane?"

I nodded, watching the boat get closer. It looked like the same two guys who'd come out with Kim and Marty the previous day. The two who looked like twins except for their eye color, Sinclair and Mahoney.

"Go get 'em," Rusty said, moving toward the conning tower. "We came up here to install 'em to help keep the sub's batteries charged."

Billy followed after him. "There is no way to hook those up. We would need an inverter and—"

"They don't know that," Rusty snapped. "We'll just run the wires down through the hatch and pretend to hook 'em up."

I didn't figure it was necessary but went back to the plane to get the panels anyway. Kim and Marty had vouched for the two officers, and that was good enough for me. But this was Rusty's gig and he didn't trust anyone he didn't know. And that much gold, if known about, was one hell of an enticement.

As we'd loaded the gold on the plane, we'd all agreed to keep the find a secret until we could ascertain who to return it to. Normally, finding gold or other shiny objects in the water was finders-keepers, but this was likely going to be a whole lot different.

The gold we'd found was likely part of the looted and liquidated assets of war-torn Europe.

I always carried two flexible, fifty-watt solar panels in *Island Hopper* that I could lay across the wing and plug into her charging system for those rare occasions when I took anglers deep into the Backcountry or the Glades for extended periods.

The lights on the FWC boat turned off as it got close enough to distinguish faces. They were just coming alongside as I pulled the two panels out and carried them to the conning tower where Rusty and Billy were waiting.

"Just lay 'em there on the deck," Rusty said, climbing down the ladder a few steps from the observation platform. "I'll plug 'em in."

"Are y'all about finished?" the brown-eyed Mahoney asked.

"Just gotta hook these up," Rusty called down from above. "Should help keep the batteries charged up while we ain't here."

Sinclair fended the boat away from the sub's hull. "Solar panels on a 1940s submarine?"

"The batteries and electric motors are modern," Rusty replied, looping both connections around the first rung of the ladder. "We installed those before moving here. And this inverter we just put in is brand-spankin' new too." He paused and patted the underside of the deck, playing it up, then climbed out of the hatch. "That oughta do her. It's readin' almost forty watts goin' in with the sun about to set. Should be plenty durin' the day."

He carefully lowered the hatch, leaving it undogged, then put the padlock back onto the hasps he'd welded in place soon after Billy found the sub.

"It has a modern power supply?" Sinclair pressed.

"Not completely," Rusty replied. "Just the electric motors and enough battery power for about thirty minutes of runnin' time. She'd need a lot more, plus new diesels, to be anywhere close to bein' operational."

"How'd it survive the elements?" Mahoney asked, seeming quite interested. "It should be a rusted heap."

"The primordial ooze at the bottom," Billy explained. "Over time, it sank deep into the mud and became covered with it. The water level in the Glades used to be much higher and we think the mud, under the pressure of deeper water, preserved the steel hull by squeezing the oxygen out from around the hull."

"So are y'all coming back tomorrow?" Mahoney asked.

"It's doubtful," Rusty said. "We ain't got much to do until some parts are made. That's why we added the solar. Now we don't have to come out every few days and run the generator."

Mahoney nodded. "Good thinking. Even with everything turned off, an old steel hull like that's going to discharge some amperage into the surrounding water."

Rusty'd sold him on the ruse.

"We saw you fly over as we were heading out," Sinclair said, turning toward me. "Seaplanes back in here seem a little suspect, so we hurried out to see what was going on."

"Float plane," I corrected him. "Seaplanes don't need to be adapted to land on water. And your suspicion is understandable. But I, and a few other backwater fishing outfits, fly out here with anglers quite often." I gave him a half-grin. "Not as rare as you'd think, but I could see where you might think it could be a drug plane or something. You guys only get to see the bad side of humans, so I'd imagine *everything's* suspect."

Mahoney shrugged. "It feels that way sometimes."

"Is that what you do?" Sinclair asked me. "You're a fishing guide?"

"I own a string of charter dive and fishing boats," I replied. "Along with two planes."

"There won't be any suspicious people out here tonight," Mahoney said. "It's just gonna be a long, boring twelve hours."

"Twelve?" I asked. "I thought you guys were doing six-hour shifts."

"That was the plan," Sinclair said. "But Kendrick, one of the guys on the midnight-to-dawn watch, has a kid in the hospital, so we're pulling a double."

"Then we'll leave ya to get at it," Rusty said. "My wife's gonna have supper on the table just about the time we get back."

Billy looked toward the setting sun. "And if I am to get home before nightfall, I'd better get moving as well."

"Oh, hey," Sinclair said. "Hang on a sec."

He moved quickly to the foredeck and opened a storage bin, then pulled out a can of kerosene and a brand-new lantern. "Can you get this back to your friend? And here's a full can, to replace the one we opened. I got four more."

Rusty glanced at the very stern of the sub, where Jimmy's lantern hung on a twisted and broken rail, the open can of fuel beside it.

"I reckon it worked out pretty good then?" Rusty asked, accepting the can and heading toward the lantern.

"With red LEDs in the boat," Mahoney began, "we didn't have a single bug all night. Just sat and listened to music, a coupla podcasts, and did some work on some old open cases."

"Anythin' interestin'?" Rusty asked, putting the lantern and half-full kerosene can in the plane. "My wife's kind of a forensics and cold case junky."

"There's one that's baffled us for over a year," Mahoney said. "A few miles south of here, a fisherman came across the wreck of an airboat that looked like it'd suffered a catastrophic fuel explosion, but not recently. No people, no belongings, no clues, and where it was found was way too far from *anywhere* to have drifted."

CHAPTER TWENTY-ONE

As *Island Hopper* climbed over the sawgrass, water, and scattered cypress heads, I wondered about what Mahoney had said. I could tell by his expression that Rusty was thinking the same thing.

Not long after Billy found the sub, the three of us had rigged a flexible caisson around the conning tower and pumped the water out to gain access to the hatch.

While Rusty'd been down inside the sub checking it out, we came under attack. Several people on an airboat opened fire as soon as we spotted them racing toward us, but too far away for them to have any kind of accuracy.

But not too far for the rifle I'd had in the plane that day. When I fired at the guy driving the boat, I either missed or the bullet went through him, hitting and igniting the high-octane aviation gas in the tank behind him.

The airboat had blown apart with such force there was little left of those who'd been aboard it, and the twisted wreckage sank quickly.

We still didn't know why they'd attacked.

Could the slow-moving River of Grass have carried the remnants of the airboat over the bottom that far in three years? The Glades were mostly covered with sawgrass, but there were hundreds, maybe thousands of open patches of water, twisting creeks where the majority of the water flowed at a virtual snail's pace.

"What are you going to do with the gold when we get there?" Larry asked over the intercom from the backseat.

"Find something we can put it in and sink it," I replied. "Up under the house."

"Good choice," Rusty agreed. "Whatta ya got that'll hold that much weight? And just how do you figure on liftin' it?"

"Feel like putting out some lobster traps?" I replied. "More than one, obviously."

"Perfect!" Larry exclaimed. "They can hold seventy or eighty pounds each, and we have two dozen just sitting there."

"Set 'em all in the deepest part," Rusty suggested. "They can soak there for a few days until we can arrange transport and figure out where it needs to go." He paused for a moment, then said, "Odd story Mahoney told about that blown-up airboat."

"It sure is," Larry said. "That area's so remote, any airboat out there wouldn't have had enough gas left to get back."

Rusty was curious about it, same as me. But Larry didn't know the circumstances and might not understand. In his world most people were nice and even polite.

In *my* world, however, when someone started shooting at me, they went down hard and fast, with as much violence as I could lay on them. I didn't even want their *ghosts* to get back up.

My old friend Tank Tankersley used to say that any man who needed killing was worth the investment of a second round, and if there was any doubt, empty the magazine.

Not something you talked openly about in polite society.

I leveled off at fifteen-hundred feet just as we passed over the coast, heading due south. The setting sun was barely blocked by the starboard wingtip and to the east, the sky was already darkening.

"It's going to be almost dark when we reach the island," I said, checking the time. It was 1704, and sunset would be in just thirty-one minutes. "I don't like landing in the water in the dark."

"You got a better idea?" Rusty asked. "'Cause I'm all ears."

I glanced back at the small stack of gold, covered by the blanket, trying to imagine it stacked neatly. It probably wouldn't take up as much space as a large loaf of bread.

"My hangar," I replied. "It'll be just as safe there, so long as nobody knows about it."

"Yeah, that could work," Rusty said. "Nobody can get in the gate without a pass, and your hangar's locked up with an alarm. You sure you don't wanna just go to your island?"

"Water landings are bad enough," I replied. "At night or in bad weather, risk goes up exponentially."

Rusty looked back at the blanket covering the gold. "Got a good hidin' spot there?"

"There's a plastic Igloo cooler in the corner," I said. "Next to my tool chest. It leaks already."

"I'll give Billy a call and let him know the change in plans," Rusty said, pulling his phone out.

"Do me a favor and call Savvy, too. She's expecting us there."

He nodded as he held the phone to his ear under his headset. After a short conversation with Billy, he called Savannah and told her the same thing.

He listened for a few seconds, then lowered the phone. "She wants to know how you and Larry are gonna get home. Ya wanna take my boat?"

I nodded as the sun disappeared over the horizon. Then I

turned the plane slightly east, lining up with the western end of the Seven Mile Bridge. "Tell her I'll be there in an hour, then."

He relayed the message, then ended the call. "She said not to hurry. She and Lauren are just startin' dinner."

After a few minutes, I gave my position and intentions on the unicom frequency, and entered the upwind leg to Marathon Airport.

I could see by the water that the typical easterly wind was light. After reducing the throttle, I lowered the flaps, and when the speed dropped below one hundred miles per hour, I lowered the landing gear.

All four green lights came on, indicating that the wheels in the front and rear of each float were down and locked.

We flew over the landing threshold, still a hundred feet above it, and I had the nose aiming for the middle of the runway. *Island Hopper* only needed a couple of hundred yards to slow, even without braking, and taxiing used a lot more fuel than gliding.

The wheels touched down and I reduced power further without touching the brakes. *Island Hopper* slowed quickly, and we were down to just ten miles per hour with half a football field of runway ahead of us.

My hangar was the second one just off the end taxiway, and I gunned the engine as I pushed on the left rudder pedal to turn *Island Hopper* around right in front of the big sliding doors.

Once we had the plane backed in beside her big sister, *Ocean Hopper*, I pulled one sliding door closed, then the other. The cooler was the perfect spot and was only a few feet from the cargo hatch on the plane. I opened the lid, and Rusty and Larry started passing gold bars to me in quick succession.

Finally, I closed the cooler and straightened my back as I

stood. "It totally crushed the bottom, but I think this will do for now."

Rusty moved two one-gallon oil jugs on top of the cooler, along with a funnel. "I still think it'd be safer at your island. They ain't nobody here to watch it."

"That ship's sailed," I said, glancing up at the camera over the inside of the door.

There were three of them. Besides the one over the door, there was another at the back of the hangar and one outside. The little red dots on the two interior cameras were on, meaning they were actively recording.

I grinned at Rusty. "It'll keep just fine, right here."

He looked around the hangar. "I don't know, bro. Thirty-three million in gold, and nothing but a padlock and a cheap alarm system."

"I wouldn't call it *cheap*," I replied, as we walked out through the smaller door. "Tony installed it, and it's tied in with Deuce's monitoring system." I paused, looked up at the unblinking red eye of the exterior camera and waved at it. "Hey, Chyrel."

The outside light flicked off and on twice.

CHAPTER TWENTY-TWO

We had to walk from the airport to the Rusty Anchor, but it wasn't far, barely as long as Rusty's driveway. The fact that we'd just stashed roughly thirty-three-million-dollars-worth of gold in my hangar and were forced to walk home seemed woefully at odds.

We trotted across the southbound lanes of US-1, through the median, and had to wait a moment for the northbound side to clear. Then we were quickly enveloped by Rusty's jungle, the dense foliage blocking out the traffic noise after just thirty or forty feet.

Though the sky was still light to the west, the sun wasn't visible in the wetland part of Rusty's property even at high noon.

The warmth of the day was slipping, but the humidity was still high, causing a bead of cold sweat to trickle down my back as we came out into the parking area. Or maybe it was the thought of thirty-three million in gold stashed in a cooler in my hangar.

There were four cars in the lot, besides mine and Rusty's daily drivers and his loaner car, plus the usual number of skiffs at the small dock, nearly all familiar to me.

Rusty's pickup was in its usual spot under one side of the giant live oak, with my International backed in a little crookedly under the opposite branches. His latest loaner was another in a long line of Keys cars he'd bought and allowed liveaboards to run into the ground, this one a rusting Dodge sedan, which was parked beside his truck.

The four other vehicles—two more Keys cars, Dink's old pickup, and a newer model Toyota SUV, were all parked together.

The two Keys cars belonged to liveaboards at the marina, but the SUV was unknown to me.

Tuesdays were normally slow at the Rusty Anchor, mostly local people, and this evening looked to be the same.

"Got time for a beer?" Rusty asked, angling toward the bar's door.

"I wish we could," Larry said, looking up from his phone as we entered the bar behind Rusty. "But Lauren just texted me. Dinner's in thirty minutes, or we eat leftovers and have to fight Tank for them."

Rusty chuckled as he went behind the bar, then entered the office and grabbed a set of keys off the wall.

He handed them to Larry. "Give her a minute to warm up. I need a word with Jesse."

I looked around. Bob was behind the bar, and Mitzi and John sat across from him with a new guide Dink was training. There were two couples I'd never seen sitting at a table. The sunburned noses of the two men gave them away as tourists. It didn't matter what time of year, there were always visitors in the Keys, but they usually didn't find the Rusty Anchor on a Tuesday night by accident.

Though the place filled up Thursday through Sunday, Rusty drew the line at having any kind of sign or billboard out by the road. If someone heard about his place from someone else, he wanted them to find it, and remember the hunt.

The four at the bar watched us as Rusty and I followed Larry out the back door without a word.

A young couple sat in the darkness at one of the tables on the deck, seemingly deep in conversation. Neither of them even noticed us as we walked down the steps to the lawn.

Larry continued on toward the dock and I followed Rusty around the corner, out of earshot of the deck.

Rusty stopped and turned toward me. "It was them, wasn't it?" he asserted in a low tone. "They found that damned blow boat."

"They fired first," I reminded him. "Besides, after all this time, there's nothing left that could possibly link it to us."

He looked up at the nearly full moon, now halfway up the eastern sky, and let out a deep sigh. "That's all you gotta tell yourself, bro?"

I turned toward the rum shack and looked out over the water beyond the seawall. "That and a hundred other justifications," I replied softly. "I never go looking for fights."

"I know," he said, sighing again as he turned to face me. "I didn't really mean to bring it up. You, uh... you best get goin' before Savvy tans your hide."

Rusty probably knew me better than anyone else, except maybe Savannah. During the four years he'd served, he'd been deployed with me to Okinawa for a year, and later to Beirut, Lebanon for four months as part of a multi-national peacekeeping force. That was the closest Rusty'd ever come to combat. We'd had each other's backs through numerous bar fights and outside the Corps, quite a few encounters with criminals of all sorts.

I'd lost track of the number of men I'd killed after twelve. But he knew their ghosts sometimes tormented me at night.

"I'll come down in the morning," I offered. "Bring your boat back and we can look at whatever Herman's come up with."

"See ya then," he said, turning back toward the bar.

I continued down to where Rusty's boat idled quietly beside

the barge. Larry had the lines untied and just looped around two deck cleats, the bitter ends in his hands.

I stepped down into the boat and took the lines from him. "*You* take us home," I said. "Let's see how your memory is. Rusty doesn't have a plotter."

We switched places, and when I pushed the bow away, Larry put the outboard in forward, turning toward the long row of boats on either side of the canal, and started idling toward open water.

I got the fenders up and stowed on the aft deck, then coiled the lines before returning to the helm as Larry threaded the boat out into Vaca Key Bight, nudging the throttle up slightly as we cleared land.

"How long have you lived here?" Larry asked, turning slowly toward a spot half a mile off Sister Rock.

Party Island lay dead ahead about three miles beyond it.

"My first night here with Rusty," I began, reminiscing, "was an evening just like this, about a month earlier in the year. I was seventeen and Rusty's girlfriend at the time, Julie's mom, Juliet, was driving Rusty's boat to Party Island, just ahead. Almost twenty years later, I left the Corps and came here to stay. I even bought the island and *Gaspar's Revenge* that first summer. That was in 1999."

"It's easy to understand why," he said, making no move to increase speed. "Especially why you bought your island. At first, I dreaded the boat ride back and forth to work, but now, it's one of the best parts of my day." He looked over and I could see the smile on his face from the light of the stars. "Especially the ride home after dark."

He had something else on his mind. We were in water that was five- to-eight feet deep, with nothing ahead but the Seven Mile Bridge and Moser channel.

But it's hard to talk over a screaming outboard and the rush of water, and Larry wanted to talk about something.

I simply leaned back on the post and watched the dark water slip past, giving him time to arrange his thoughts.

I had a feeling I knew what was coming.

"There's this kid in my class at the school," he began. "He, uh... had a hard childhood. Know what I mean?"

"Lauren told me some time ago," I said. "If it's the same kid. She also told me what you suspected."

He glanced over quickly at me, then back at the water ahead. "It's no longer a suspicion, Jesse."

"I see.... What do you want to do?"

He was quiet for a moment; his stoic gaze fixed on the high arch of the bridge ahead and the lights of cars passing over it.

"I want to bring him out to the island," he replied, turning the wheel slightly and lining up with the fifth bridge piling past the channel. "I'm worried the guy will come after him."

"What guy?" I asked without thinking. "I mean, who is he to the boy?"

Larry paused, as if considering what he could divulge. He made a show of looking around at the water ahead. A delay tactic; he was lined up correctly and there wouldn't be any lobster trap floats to avoid.

"When he was little," he finally replied, "a sicko drug-dealer his mom used." He paused again, then looked over at me. "More recently, his wrestling coach at the middle school he used to go to."

CHAPTER TWENTY-THREE

The next morning started like most others on the island. The forecast said a front would push down later in the day, bringing rain, northwesterly winds, and cooler-than-normal temperatures.

Old Man Winter blowing down across the Plains and the Gulf.

Even though I was still tired, I was awake before El Sol even thought about making an appearance.

I'd stayed up late talking with Larry after dinner and he'd told me that the school the boy had attended before coming to *our* school on Grassy Key was up on the mainland, in Liberty City, a part of Miami known for gangs and violent crime. Some said that living in the area between the glitz and glamor of downtown Miami and the suburbs of North Miami was akin to living in a combat zone.

I assumed those who'd repeated such nonsense had never seen combat.

It was one thing to run the risk of being the victim of a street crime in a bad neighborhood, and quite another when you walked through a village with absolute knowledge that every pair of eyes that looked your way would be someone who would kill you if you let down your guard even for a second.

Those thoughts were already on my mind as I quietly rose from the bed to let Savannah sleep in.

Tank met me in the living room, and after we went down to ground level and performed our morning rituals, I walked around the whole island with him.

It wasn't something we normally did, and for the first half, Tank seemed eager, as if expecting me to do or say something, or maybe teach him some new skill, but I just wanted to think.

Grassy Key was a two-and-a-half-hour drive from Liberty City.

The idea of a grown man molesting a kid, boy or girl, was revolting and made my blood boil. The fact that he was a wrestling coach, a position of great authority and admiration to an adolescent, compounded it immensely.

I remembered all my coaches with respect. I was closer to some than others, but every coach I'd had all through Little League, junior high, and high school were... well, manly men. Like a dad or favorite uncle, but someone with single-minded focus: to mold boys into young men, young men into athletes, and athletes into teams. They got emotional when their team did well, and angry when they didn't. But no coach I'd ever known had ever hit a kid or touched them in any way than as a father or mentor would.

When Tank and I completed our circuit, Tank followed me past the house and out to the end of the south pier. He was a smart dog, maybe the most intelligent animal I'd ever known, but more than that, he was extremely intuitive. He seemed to understand the reason for our walk before we'd passed the bunk houses.

He sat down beside me on the pier, ears up, panting softly with a jowly Lab grin on his face.

A two-and-a-half-hour drive, I thought again, glancing back at the big doors covering the dock area under the house. Add a half hour to get from the island to the Rusty Anchor. I looked at my watch. It was 0530. I could be in Liberty City before the first bell rang.

And do what? I chastised myself.

The media would have a field day.

FLORIDA MAN ATTACKS RESPECTED SCHOOL TEACHER

Film at eleven.

Besides, an ass-whipping wouldn't change those people. No pedophile was ever truly rehabilitated. Not even after becoming some other inmate's "girlfriend" for twenty years.

Prisoners had a strong abhorrence for men who abused children, and pedophiles introduced to the prison population became punching bags on day one and a sex toy before nightfall. Often, several times.

Usually, the guards turned their backs and didn't see it.

Guards and inmates had kids too.

The problem was, the only way to put these turd fondlers behind bars where they belonged would be if a victim came forward, identified the pedophile, and there was enough evidence for a conviction.

That rarely happened.

Sitting on the end of the pier, letting my bare feet dangle a few inches above the water, I looked out across Harbor Channel. It was almost low tide. At high tide, the water would be above my ankles.

"Should I just kill him?" I asked Tank softly.

He turned his big head and looked at me, the light of a billion stars reflecting in his dark brown eyes. Then he made a soft puppy sound, stretched his paws out, and laid his head on my thigh.

"Kill who?" Savannah asked, coming up quietly behind us.

Tank lifted his head for a moment, looked back, then slapped the deck twice with his tail and dropped his head back onto my lap.

She handed me a coffee mug, then sat down beside Tank with hers as I started to explain what I'd learned from Larry the previous night.

"Dying's too easy," she said. "We'll just find a way to get him arrested for it. That shouldn't be too hard to do."

"I'd just as soon put a bullet in—"

"I know," she interrupted, leaning her head on my shoulder. "But you can't. It's much too risky, right in the middle of the city. But there are things far worse than—"

My phone buzzed in my pocket, startling both of us. There was a time when I didn't have one, and when I finally broke down and got one, I lost or misplaced it all the time, often in odd places like my tackle box, the engine room on the *Revenge*, or in the fridge. I lost two in the first year.

These days, I was rarely without one—I had three—but calls on my private phone before sunrise were rare.

After pulling it out, I checked the screen. "It's Kim," I said, then stabbed the *Accept* button with my finger. Putting it to my ear, I mustered a cheerful voice. "This is early, even for you. What's up?"

"My two officers are dead," she stated flatly. "That's what the hell is *up*, Dad."

CHAPTER TWENTY-FOUR

From the reports Kim had received from the officers who'd arrived early to relieve Mahoney and Sinclair, the two men had both been shot multiple times, and it appeared neither had even had time to draw a sidearm.

Mahoney and Sinclair had been out there in Whitewater Bay since before sunset, pulling a double shift they expected to be dull and boring, so a fellow officer could be with his kid in the hospital.

It had all the earmarks of a well-planned ambush, except for one huge fact. How the hell could anyone get the drop on two seasoned cops, on a boat, in the middle of an inland bay, miles from anything?

I knew from experience that as far out in the Glades as the sub was, it was extremely quiet at night, with the nearest road of any kind being forty or fifty miles away.

Billy and I had spent quite a few nights out in the Corkscrew Swamp and in the Everglades. Sometimes, we heard airboat engines far in the distance, and Billy had told me that his father, William "Leaping Panther" Rainwater had said he'd often measured the distance he and his buddies could hear one another's airboats using CB radios. Often, the sound could be heard further away than the radios could transmit.

And an airboat or float plane was about the only way to get to Whitewater Bay, unless someone came in off the Gulf, like the

FWC guys had. That would mean an outboard, which could also be heard from a considerable distance.

"Do you need me to come there?" I asked Kim, knowing I'd have to explain to her about the gold.

Once was puzzling. Twice was no coincidence. What else could the killers have been after?

Somebody knew about the gold.

"Later, for sure," Kim replied. "You'll just be in the way now. The ME and forensics teams are on the way out there, and Marty's getting my boat ready. But you, Rusty, and Billy need to come back out to give a statement about anything missing and secure the scene once the forensics techs are finished. Corporal Troutman reported that the hatch on the submarine was open."

That was *not* good. Whoever it was, they knew there was something on that sub that was worth killing two armed police officers over. But how?

Then it suddenly hit me. Herman's internet research. He was being digitally tracked.

"I have to take Rusty's boat back down to Marathon," I said. "He and I will head over to the airport and get *Island Hopper* ready and wait for your call. We can be there an hour later, and Billy's about an hour away, too."

"There's no rush, Dad," Kim said. I could feel the weight of responsibility in her voice. "We'll be there most of the day and will have double security going forward. Marty contacted the sheriff, and they'll be reinforcing us. Sheriff Ramsey promised to put a "bee under DNR's hat" to move up the lock construction. Everyone wants that thing out of the Glades. It's even been suggested that the attack might have been an act of eco-terrorism."

"Eco-terror—"

"I gotta go, Dad," she said suddenly. "Marty's ready."

I ended the call and drained the cold remnants of my mug down my throat before turning to Savannah. "I guess you heard most of that."

"You have to tell her, Jesse. And you have to turn over that gold."

I had to assume three things. First, whoever had attacked the FWC officers guarding the sub had to have known about the gold, or at least knew there was *something* of value aboard. The alternative would be that it was a random attack, or it was carried out for some other reason. I wasn't buying eco-terrorists. We were moving the sub *out* of the Glades, not in.

Besides, it was the second attack.

Regardless of motive, the question remained. How did they surprise Mahoney and Sinclair?

My second assumption was that they didn't know where the gold was currently located. At least not immediately after failing to find it on the sub. But it wouldn't take long for them to figure it out or at least determine who had control of it.

Rusty was the salvor, a matter of public record, available to anyone.

Lastly, I had to assume that last night's attack was somehow connected to the one just over two years ago. How or why, I didn't know, but we'd considered the submarine fairly safe way out there. At least safe against handguns or rifles. An RPG or depth charge would likely be a different story. So, if whoever attacked us the first time knew about the gold, they either hadn't told anyone else, which now seemed unlikely, or hadn't divulged the location. We figured it was electronic tracking back then, and it looked like the same now. Herman's searches had tipped somebody off that the gold was still out there.

I'd seen Chyrel use the technology a few times—simple search term flags that pointed out someone doing specific internet searches—versus someone making random searches about submarines.

"I'll get Rusty's boat ready to go," Savannah said, getting to her feet. "You call him and Billy and let them know what happened."

I got quickly to my feet and followed after her with Tank at my heels. "Go with her," I told him, as Savannah started up the steps.

The only access to the boat docks below the house was a set of stairs in the living room and the big doors on the outside. Tank would follow her up, down, into the boat, and out to the dock.

I went around the corner to the dry storage closet under the steps and opened it. Behind the panel in back, I retrieved my Sig and holster, clipping it onto my belt and dropping an extra magazine in my pocket.

Then I got my phone out and called Rusty first. Billy's plane was right in his backyard, and he could get to Whitewater Bay in a matter of minutes. In his airboat, he could still be there in under an hour.

"What's wrong?" Rusty asked urgently when he answered.

"There's been a development," I told him. "We need to get out to the sub and meet Kim and Marty. We have to tell them about the gold, and Herman has to stop his online research."

"But he's found what we were looking—wait. What? Why're Kim and Marty out there?"

"Mahoney and Sinclair are dead," I told him, as I heard the click of the big boat doors' latch.

"Huh? How? What happened?"

I explained what little I knew, then moved on quickly to what I suspected about last night's attack being connected to the one two years ago.

I went on to tell him how Herman's internet searches must have been detected, rekindling an interest by some third party. "And you're the salvager of record," I concluded.

"Okay, okay," he said with an edge to his voice. "You head on down here and we'll fly up there in your plane."

"We have to wait for Kim to call," I said. "The Monroe County Sheriff's forensics team is on their way, along with the medical examiner."

"We're screwed," he declared in an exasperated tone, a state I'd never seen him in. "Totally screwed. Don't matter what they find. The first question's gonna be about why those solar panels are just layin' there not hooked up to nothin', and then why we were there all day to accomplish that."

"Exactly," I said, walking back toward the dock. "That's why we have to tell Kim about the gold."

"Herman found the rightful owners of all of it, bro," Rusty said in a somber tone. "All them fake 'crewmens'' names in the logbook? They all had one thing in common. They were all commanders of different outfits of the German occupation forces in Amsterdam, right up until September of 1944, when they all just up and disappeared without a trace."

CHAPTER TWENTY-FIVE

As Savannah pulled Rusty's boat out from under the house, I made my second call. Being to Billy, that one was much shorter and to the point. I explained what happened, and what the situation now was in a short, concise manner.

"I agree," he said. "Call me when you know the time. I'll be waiting at the dock and can be there in under an hour."

"I'll let you know," I promised, then ended the call.

"Do you want me to go with you?" Savannah asked, as she and Tank climbed out of the boat, leaving the outboard running.

"Alberto has lessons," I said.

"Which I'm learning right along with him," she reminded me. "He can study on his own, and Lauren will be here all day. And you haven't eaten."

"Don't worry," I said. "I'll eat at the Anchor. I want to hear what Herman came up with. We're going to tell Kim and Marty where the gold is, so they can arrange transport and storage. Herman figured out where it came from."

"Where?" she asked, as I stepped down into the boat. "And that's not why I asked if you needed me."

Looking up at her, I smiled. Savannah was on the short list of people I'd want watching my back in a dicey situation. She was more than capable with a handgun or rifle, usually very cool-headed, and over the years, had become a formidable unarmed combatant.

"Amsterdam," I replied. "All the Nazi officers on the sub were high-ranking members of the occupation forces in the city."

"Dutch Jews," she said, her face aghast.

"What those officers smuggled out of Amsterdam," I said, shaking loose the bow line, "was just a drop in a bucket to what was channeled back to Berlin."

"Be careful," she said, as I pushed away from the dock and shifted the outboard to forward.

"I will," I lied.

The truth is, I *am* a cautious man, but being overly vigilant without appearing to be, while looking the way I do, was a delicate balance.

I couldn't hide my appearance. Any man my size, who appeared capable, and acted overly wary, could sometimes trigger a sort of fight-or-flight response in certain groups of men, who then possibly became antagonistic.

I'd seen it too many times to not notice and understand. By at least *appearing* somewhat carefree on the outside often lessened the risk of some overgrown "playground bully" feeling threatened merely by my presence.

When I reached Harbor Channel, I turned left, noting the tide had risen slightly just in the last half hour. Tidal changes weren't great in the Keys, but the currents did move pretty quickly at peak flow, which was now halfway between high and low. And it was flooding, meaning a huge amount of water was flowing north through the Keys and its many cuts, channels, and passes, and eventually into the Gulf. In larger channels, like Harbor Channel and Moser Channel, where the water wasn't as restricted and was deeper, the tidal current moved more slowly. But in some of the narrow cuts and gaps, it could move at better than five or six knots. Not good when navigating a winding passage at low speed. A boat could easily be pushed up onto a bank by an eddy.

There would be a fast-flowing current through the cut just south of Mac Travis and Melody Woodson's island, as well as across the flats on either side of it. I'd be moving against the current, with the surrounding flats far too shallow for Rusty's boat.

So, when I straightened the wheel, I pushed the throttle down and headed east-northeast, toward the mouth of the channel, where it met the Gulf. There, I could circle around the flats and into Moser Channel.

The sun was almost an hour from peeking over the horizon, but the sky was already gray with the first morning light, and I could see clearly all the way out to Harbor Light.

Glancing over toward Mac and Mel's place, I didn't see any lights on, and Mac's boat wasn't tied up on the east side where he usually kept the odd-looking Munson.

I continued straight out into the Gulf of Mexico for a few minutes, then started a slow turn to the right until I was heading due south, lining the bow up with a dark patch on the horizon between the two domes of light emanating from Marathon and Big Pine Key.

Both cities, as well as the Seven Mile Bridge between them, were well over the horizon, and a good ten miles away, so no actual lights were visible, just the glow from tens of thousands of them.

I was worried about Rusty. He used a Marathon post office box for anything relating to salvage work, but he was far too well-known in the area to be anonymous. If the attack was intentional, and they were after the gold, they could find his PO box and might be able to find him.

I hadn't thought it necessary for me to warn him that someone could come gunning. Two dead cops, the possibility of electronic detection, and him being the person holding the salvage rights to the sub made him a target.

He'd take the needed precautions, and he'd probably put the word out to the folks in the marina and fishing communities to keep an eye out for anyone asking too many questions.

Rusty's big Evinrude pushed the boat effortlessly along at thirty knots, only the aft third of the boat in contact with the calm water.

In another twelve hours, a storm front would be coming through, and this open stretch to the bridge would become as agitated as a washing machine.

Ten minutes later, with the bridge astern, I made another wide turn around Sister Rock, into Vaca Key Bight, then slowed as I approached the channel to Rusty's place.

I could see lights on in a few boats, as well as in the restaurant, but I didn't see anyone moving about. I continued up the canal between the docked boats, which blocked my view, until I reached the big barge and dredging backhoe in the turning basin.

About five yards away, I killed the engine, then turned the wheel, sending the boat drifting toward the barge, where I fended it away, then stepped off with the lines in my hands.

Once I'd tied Rusty's boat off, I stood and looked around. Not a soul in sight.

It seemed almost as if everyone had left and forgotten to turn the lights off. With sunrise just ten or fifteen minutes away, there was now plenty of ambient daylight, so artificial lights weren't needed.

But they were *all* on.

I went across the gangplank to the seawall and stepped down, looking around. It appeared as if every light in Rusty's house was on, as well as the big streetlight over the door to the dry stack building behind the house.

Out beyond the buildings, the big orange light on the pole in the middle of the yard was on... even the decorative lights around the deck rails were lit up.

Trudging across the well-lit yard, I stepped up onto the small porch and reached for the doorknob.

Suddenly, the door flew open, revealing a giant of a man silhouetted against the bright lights inside.

CHAPTER TWENTY-SIX

I wasn't a man prone to being easily startled; I always tried to anticipate the unexpected. But all the lights on and nobody around had set my nerves jingling.

"Well, hey, Jesse," Dink said, a surprised look on his face as he stepped back. "You're up early."

"I could say the same for you," I replied. "But I know you've probably been up for hours already."

"Just got the last of my clients matched up with their guides," he said. "Rusty's in the office, if you're lookin' for him."

"Thanks," I said, then headed to the open end of the bar, where Mitzi sat hunched over a coffee.

Rusty's cousin, Maddy, was wiping down a table in the middle of the room and waved a hand.

"Hey, Maddy," I said. "When you get a minute, can you ask Rufus for a couple of breakfast burritos?"

"Sure thing," she replied, as I went behind the bar.

I said good morning to Mitzi, and got a nod in return. She wasn't a morning person.

Opening the door to Rusty's office, I found him seated behind his old desk, the receiver to an old rotary desk phone held to his ear.

He motioned me to sit down, so I closed the door and I took a seat in the only other chair in the small room. I could hear the voice on the phone but couldn't make out any of the words.

My eyes scanned the dozens of framed but faded photos of Rusty or his dad, Shorty, standing with notable figures, friends, and fishermen, some taken during some wild parties at the Anchor and a few wilder ones at Shorty's Bait Shop and Bar, which was what the Rusty Anchor was called when Shorty owned it.

All the photos were familiar to me and I knew the names of everyone in them, though I'd only personally met a couple. My personal favorite was an old black-and-white of Shorty and a very pregnant Dreama, Rusty's mom. It was taken in Havana, Cuba, early in the fall of 1958, just a couple of months before Rusty was born and Castro finally overthrew Batista.

In the picture, Shorty and Dreama were seated at a garden table on a stone patio with the ocean in the background and none other than Papa himself—Ernest Hemingway—seated with them.

I remembered being highly impressed the first time I'd seen it, and Shorty had explained how he and the author had become friends over rum and tales of fishing.

"Okay, then," Rusty said. "Print what ya got and bring it over. But no more internet searches."

"Herman?" I asked, as Rusty hung up the desk phone.

"Yeah," he replied. "He's got some pretty interestin' facts about the occupation of Amsterdam that he was able to make notes of."

"What kind of facts?"

"They kept records of everything," Rusty said. "The Germans, that is. They really believed in the Hundred-Year-Reich. Most of the Jewish Dutch folks living in the Netherlands were basically robbed of everything—businesses, houses, furniture, jewelry, art, silverware... you name it. Anything of value. It was all liquidated and sent to Berlin in the form of Swiss gold, just like we found."

"I guess not all of it got on the trains to Berlin," I stated.

"To the tune of over five hundred thousand *bucks*," he replied. "But that was in 1944 dollars; worth almost a hundred times that today. More than enough to get all them Nazi officers all set up in South America, smuggle their families out of Germany, and live like kings for the rest of their miserable lives."

"Any idea what happened to them?" I asked. "Their families?"

"Five of the twelve 'passengers' were wanted for war crimes," he replied. "Whatever family survived the war lived in poverty, outcast by their own people." He paused and let out a breath. "You ain't heard from Kim, I take it?"

"It'll probably be a while," I replied. "A few hours maybe."

"Them two kids?" he began. "Mahoney and Sinclair? They got family?"

"Kim said Mahoney was from up north," I replied. "Never married, no kids. Sinclair was divorced and had a son."

Rusty looked up, his eyes locked with mine. "How old?"

"She didn't say," I replied. "You're thinking what happened to them was somehow your fault? Don't do that, brother. Risk goes with the badge."

Rusty sat back in his worn chair. "Yeah, well, I bet they never busted no 'swamp chemist' with thirty-three million in crank."

"Kim said people are thinking it might've been eco-terrorists."

"Eco-terrorists?" he scoffed. "That don't make no sense at all. If anything, they'd want to contribute to get it moved out *faster*."

I grinned. "You seem pretty relaxed for someone the bad guys might already think has possession of all that gold."

He turned his computer screen around. On it were four high-resolution camera feeds. I recognized one as being the camera over the front door, aimed at the parking lot and driveway.

A second feed I knew was from the camera Rusty'd mounted

on top of the rum shack last year—the Sunset Cam. It was a live feed on his new website, along with the camera over the bar. The Sunset Cam was obviously pointed in the direction of the setting sun and showed the canal entrance and the channel approach beyond it.

The other two feeds were infrared cameras, somewhere in the woods. I could see nothing but trees, shrubs, and ferns.

"Trail cams?" I asked.

"A little more high-tech 'an *that*," he said, pointing to the display at the lower right. "This one's on the foot path over to Sombrero Beach Road and aimed that way." He moved his finger to the other feed. "And this one's just off the driveway, lookin' toward the highway. Both are wireless, solar-powered, and motion-activated, *with* night optics."

I leaned closer. The driveway camera must have been set back a few feet into the treeline and mounted low. I couldn't see the actual crushed shell driveway, but I could make out the open space and the familiar spacing of the trees.

Then it hit me. It was in the only sunny spot in the jungle, just before the last left-hand curve coming in from US-1. Someone driving or walking in would be facing the camera for several seconds.

"There's also motion sensors in the wetland area," he said. "In case someone wants to take the road less traveled."

I chuckled. "Aren't you all high-tech now. No satellite imaging?"

"That'll come after we unload the gold," he said with a wry grin. "If there's enough left after I buy a ticket on Elon's rocket ship."

I knew he was joking about both. Either one would cost more than all three of our shares combined.

It was impressive, though. All three means of ingress to the property were being monitored, and probably recorded, though few knew about the foot path, and only an idiot would try to get through the tangled mangrove roots of the wetland. But if they did, they'd have to pass in front of one of the two trail cams, then become visible to the camera over the front door.

Rusty turned the screen back to face him. "I ain't paranoid or nothin'. These are just dangerous times. I been addin' to my security system since Sid and I got hitched."

"Being paranoid doesn't mean someone *isn't* out to get you," I said.

It was his turn to chuckle. "Quotin' Sergeant Livingston now?"

"You still call him sergeant," I said. "That was a long time ago. He died two decades ago, and his son is now your son-in-law. That makes him related, right?"

"Not in this country," he replied. "In old Norse, he'd be my *svær*, or father-in-law, the same as he was Julie's. And I'd be his."

"So why do you still call him sergeant?" I persisted, since we had nothing better to talk about. "If he were still alive, you'd be family and friends. Remember when we were in Oki, he preferred we called him Russ when off duty?"

"By then you was already a corporal," Rusty countered. "It's... I dunno... just a way of showin' respect."

"Where's Sid?"

"At the gym," he replied. "Three days a week."

"I thought you went together."

"We're together almost twenty-four-seven as it is," he replied. "So we alternate days, Monday to Saturday." He grinned. "Only need one membership that way."

His attention was diverted to the computer screen, then he leaned in closer.

"Something on one of the cameras?" I asked.

He nodded. "Just Cindy Lee, pedalin' her bike in. Maddy has a dentist appointment, so Cindy's coverin' things till Sid gets back. Just in case we gotta take off real quick."

"Since you brought up the familial definition between you and Russ," I began, sitting forward with my elbows on my knees. "Have you heard back from your cousin-brother?"

"Aw, shit!" he exclaimed, sitting forward. "He's comin' here this mornin'!"

CHAPTER TWENTY-SEVEN

Apparently, Rusty and his DNA match had exchanged a few emails, then made a couple of phone calls. The guy had recently retired and moved to Lakeland, up in the middle of the state, to continue his search for his biological father. Since he'd been planning a fishing trip anyway, he'd arranged charters with a couple of Dink's guides and would be in town through the weekend.

"So what's the story, then?" I asked. "How do you have a first cousin you never knew about?"

"We ain't figured out all the details," he replied. "But remember that uncle I told ya about?"

"Your mom's brother, Chuck? You said he never had kids."

"Not that he ever knew of," Rusty replied. "I feel pretty confident about that. If he'd known he had a kid, he'd have stepped up. He always wanted a son."

I nodded. "You said he adopted?"

"Yeah, ain't that a kicker?" he replied. "He married late in life and they adopted a baby boy. Works for some state congressman up in Tallahassee now. But this guy, Hoyt, he was born when my uncle was in the Air Force in the early '50s, and stationed way out in Colorado."

"They had to meet somewhere," I said. "Colorado's as good a place as any."

He grinned. "Uncle Chuck was a straight arrow, kinda prudish, some said. But a young man far from home?" He paused. "So when I mentioned to Hoyt that he was in Colorado at that time, he tells me his birth mom, who he found years ago but has since passed away, was also in the Air Force, also stationed in Colorado, *and get this*, she was from Lake Wales."

I nodded again. "First thing two military people ask when they meet is where they're from. Sounds like they had a connection far from home. Do you remember which base?"

He gave me a puzzled look. "What difference does that make? They had to be at the same one."

"Just curious," I replied. "I think back then, there were only two or three in Colorado."

"He was stationed in Colorado Springs," Rusty replied. "I don't remember the name of the base, though. He used to tell me about the mountains when I was a kid. He was like ten years older'n Mom."

"Peterson Field," I surmised. "Strategic Air Command. That means they were both sharp airmen."

There was a knock on the door, then it opened, and Cindy leaned in. "Oh, hey, Jesse," she said, waving demurely. "I didn't know you were here. Sorry to interrupt." Then she looked at Rusty. "I just wanted to let you know I'm here now, and Maddy's leaving."

"Thanks," Rusty said. "Jesse and I might have to cut out real sudden, a business thing. Will you be okay alone? Sid'll be back by nine or nine-thirty."

"Dink and John are both here," she said. "And it looks like they've settled in for the day. It just started raining."

"Check the weather," he said. "See if that front's speeded up or somethin'. Them guys only get it right when it's a coupla hours away."

She nodded and closed the door.

"That girl's sweet on you," Rusty said, a crooked grin on his face.

"I know," I replied. It came out sounding more exasperated than I actually felt and I backpedaled it. "She's never said anything openly but I picked up on it last year. She knows I'm married and almost twice her age, too."

"Since when has either of those things meant a hill of beans?" He rose from behind the desk, and I got up with him. "If we're just gonna hang out here all mornin', I need to get some work done. C'mon, I got somethin' I wanna show ya."

I followed him out through the bar, and we stopped to say hi to Larry and a now-caffeinated Mitzi, sitting with Dink and Hannah.

"We're talking about a cruise," Hannah said, bubbling with excitement. "John and Mitzi want to go to Belize and need crew, and I want to take Dink there."

"Been there twice," I said. "Terrific flats fishing; permit, bonefish, snook, jacks… even tarpon."

"C'mon," Rusty said. "Out to the garage."

I followed him outside and around the back corner of the restaurant, angling past his house toward the left side of the big metal building. The right side housed the dry storage for boats, stacked on racks with a giant forklift.

But the left side, maybe a fourth of the total building, was Rusty's personal garage space, where he worked on his hotrod, and occasionally other peoples' cars, as well as boats and outboards of all kinds.

He had about two thousand square feet on that side and was

currently restoring a 1920s-era motor launch, which once shuttled wealthy guests to some rich guy's yacht in New York Harbor.

The hull was oak planking below the waterline, fastened with brass rivets to heavy oak ribs and brass floors, with cedar planks from the waterline to the rails. It had a small, Ford four-cylinder gas engine, mass-produced for the Model T, that once supplied twenty horsepower but was seized up now. The boat was designed and built in New England to carry up to fourteen passengers in comfort and style.

Rusty figured he could restore it and either sell it to one of the sunset cruise companies in Key West or use it as a shuttle, like he did with the Tiki taxi.

He unlocked the small door next to the big roll-up, opened it, then stepped inside and turned on the lights. The boat took up half of the left side of the large bay, with Rusty's Fairlane parked behind it.

"That's the only light you *didn't* have on," I noted.

"No windows in here," he replied, walking toward a wrecked forklift. "Check this out."

The thing had obviously toppled over, probably off a loading dock, damaging the forks and riser mechanism, and crushing the cage. But it didn't appear it was damaged to the point of pinning anyone inside.

"A beat-up old forklift?" I asked, admiring the work that'd been done on the boat's hull.

"A beat-up, *one-year-old* forklift," he said. "With an *electric* motor."

I turned to look at the wreck. "How big?"

"Twenty-five kilowatts," he stated flatly. "And I think I can use the transmission out of it, too. Just have to get a custom-made prop shaft."

A twenty-kilowatt electric motor was roughly equivalent to a thirty-four-horsepower engine, which was a good bit more power than the original Model T motor, but still small by today's standards for a twenty-six-foot inboard launch.

I looked at my watch. It was almost 0700 and I knew Kim wasn't going to call for at least two hours. It'd take that long for the ME to get out there. And I figured Rusty and I both could use a diversion to get our minds off of the reason she'd be calling.

"An hour," I said. "Then we should clean up and be ready."

CHAPTER TWENTY-EIGHT

We didn't get a whole lot done in an hour—just the removal of the twisted cage and the side and rear panels to get access to the electric motor and transmission.

As we were cleaning up, something occurred to me. "You're not going to be able to use that transmission," I said. "It has to be geared way too low for a boat."

"Ya know, I was just thinkin' that same thing," he replied. "A gas-powered forklift at full speed don't go much faster than a trot."

"Probably has a two- or maybe even three-to-one reduction gear," I agreed. "You'll want no lower than one-to-one. Think the transmission in the boat's any good?"

He turned and looked back. "I never checked. Figured if the motor's seized up, no modern engine's gonna match up to the gearbox anyway."

Just then, the door behind us opened and we both turned quickly.

A man in his late sixties or early seventies stood in the doorway. He wore his gray hair long, pulled back in a thick ponytail, sported a long, gray goatee and wore glasses.

"Is one of you Rusty Thurman?" he asked. "The young lady at the bar said I'd find him back here."

"I'm Rusty. Are you Hoyt?"

The man nodded and stepped into the garage a few feet. Unlike Rusty, he was tall. Probably six feet or more, and though he was big around the middle, he carried it well. At first glance, he looked like one of those guys from Championship Wrestling from Florida way back in the day, but not seeing Gordon Solie with him, I figured Rusty's guess was correct, and he was meeting a cousin for the first time.

"Hoyt Cooper," the man said, smiling broadly.

They met in the middle and shook hands, then embraced one another. I stood back, pretending to examine something on the forklift motor.

"This's my good friend, Jesse," Rusty said. "Jesse, this here's my cousin, Hoyt."

I stepped forward and shook hands with him. He had big hands, but I could tell it wasn't from hard labor, and he didn't attempt the death grip like some men do. My guess was that he was a retired salesman, corporate executive, or something like that.

"Me and Jesse known each other a long time," Rusty said, sounding a bit nervous. "Neither of us have siblings, so we're kinda like brothers."

"Which begs the question," I said, my curiosity getting the best of me. "Rusty's second cousin here in the Keys, who he's known since she was born, also took that test. She's only a three-percent match, and my math tells me a first cousin should be a twelve percent match. You two are fourteen. Have y'all figured *that* out yet?"

"I'm an accountant," Hoyt said. "I work a lot with numbers and have been doing this DNA thing for a few years, trying to find my biological parents. You're right. A first cousin is usually a 12.5

percent match, or one-eighth, since there are eight people involved."

"Eight?" I asked with a crooked grin. "I thought it only took two."

He laughed, and I could hear Rusty's mirth in his tone.

"You have two cousins," he explained, holding up the index and middle fingers of his left hand. "Between them, they have four parents, two of which are siblings." He counted out four more digits. "That's six people, and since two of the parents are siblings, first cousins share common grandparents, which is the definition of a first cousin. So there's eight involved in the creation of the two first cousins."

"Jesse already figured out the math part," Rusty said. "But it's still a mystery."

"There could be two reasons for our match being higher," Hoyt continued. "The first is called genetic recombination, where a child gets slightly more or less DNA from one parent or grandparent than another. But that rarely gets higher than a 13.8-percent match."

"What's the other way?" Rusty asked.

"You could be cousins in more than one branch," I told him. "First on one side, plus third on another, or double second cousins, or third and first."

"Exactly," Hoyt said, snapping his finger, another trait Rusty often exhibited. "Through DNA, I learned that I was first cousin to someone in the Thurman clan. I'd found and talked with many second and third cousins, but it wasn't until Rusty took the test that I was certain. We are first cousins through his mother's brother, Willard Cooper."

"Nobody called him that," Rusty said. "I didn't even know it was his real first name until I got married. Everyone called him Chuck."

"You study genealogy?" Hoyt asked me. "You seem to have a better-than-average grasp."

"He's a numbers guy, too," Rusty said. "And he's got a photographic memory."

"I'm a retired Marine and current charter service owner," I replied. "Rusty told me you booked a couple of his guides. If you'd like to get offshore, I can set something up."

"Today's Wednesday," Rusty said. "You don't charter on weekends, and I know you're booked solid three weeks out."

"It won't be a charter," I said. "Let's call it a family fishing trip."

"Oh, hey," Rusty said, turning back to his cousin. "That reminds me...we're waitin' for a call from Jesse's daughter. Something came up early this mornin', and we might need to fly up to the Everglades just about any time now."

"The Everglades?" Hoyt asked, turning toward me. "She *lives* there?"

"She's a cop," I replied, watching his eyes. "Late last night, there was an attack on the security people who were guarding a boat Rusty's been salvaging. Two men were killed."

CHAPTER TWENTY-NINE

The boat was overdue. If all had gone according to plan, it should have arrived before sunrise. All they had to do was go to the location Manish had learned the submarine had been moved to, arrive after midnight, and find the gold. He'd even told them where to start looking.

Manish detested working with men who were all brawn and no brain. But the fact that the submarine would be guarded didn't seem to matter to the mercenary Manish had been assigned to work with. In their line of work, two guards meant only that they needed four men or more.

Several months earlier, Manish had found a letter deep in the German archives. It was from the submarine's captain, Hans Crittenden, and written to his wife. He'd sent it just before he and many high-ranking officers in the German occupation army left Amsterdam for Argentina.

She, like his commanding officer as well as his crew, thought he and a handful of other officers had gone down with the ship after an aerial bombardment.

After the war, he'd been named a wanted war criminal, and she'd hoped that releasing the letter might remove that stigma his name carried—the name she and their children also bore.

In the letter, Hans Crittenden had outlined how he and several others were escaping Germany ahead of the eventual overthrow by

Allied forces, and he would arrange to get her and the children out as soon as he was set up in Argentina.

As a peculiar sidenote, he'd told her not to worry, they'd welded the torpedo tubes shut in case they were captured. He'd said it would show they had left Germany to *escape* Hitler, not to attack shipping.

Manish was certain that was where the gold had been hidden—in the torpedo tubes.

As he looked down the creek toward open water, he considered the man who was heading the salvage operation, James Thurman. Keeping the discovery of a submarine secret for more than two years was one thing, but a fortune in gold was totally different.

The salvor had seemed to be doing everything by the law. At least on paper. Manish knew they'd found the submarine some time ago, as had the Crittenden grandsons, Karl and Lucas. Had they relayed the location to Manish, instead of going after the treasure for themselves, they'd likely still be alive today, and probably a good deal richer.

He'd sent the three siblings, Wilem, Kevin, and Lena Crittenden, the great-grandchildren of the submarine's captain, down to Marathon, to locate and watch the salvor. But all he could give them was a box number at the Marathon post office.

He hadn't yet told them about the circumstances surrounding the deaths of their father and uncle. Only that they'd disappeared trying to find the treasure. That should have been enough for them to understand that they shouldn't try to find out anything more than where the salvor lived.

If Thurman, who by all accounts was following the letter of the law, *had* actually found the gold, it would be known. Of that, Manish felt certain. It was far too much to be fenced in any usual fashion. And the salvor likely wouldn't know of less scrupulous ways of liquidating a hard asset like gold.

He'd only sent the siblings there as a precaution and to try to get ahead of the game if the mercenaries didn't come through.

The location of the submarine was only forty miles from where Manish waited. He'd rented a heavy-duty cargo van the previous evening and had driven across the state to be closer to what was going on and to facilitate delivery to his employer.

If the amount of gold was what he thought it was going to be, he was going to take his ten percent and retire. Just forget about all this research, digging through dusty archives, chasing one dead-end lead after another, and especially having to work with dodgy characters like *Mister* Damien.

The man was a brute and a barbarian, only minimally restrained by their mutual employer. And quite full of himself, that was certain.

Far in the distance, Manish heard what sounded like a boat. He looked at his phone again. It was almost eight o'clock.

The mercenary had messaged him at one in the morning, saying that it had taken some time to locate the target, and they were going to have to move in stealthily from a distance.

That was seven hours ago, he thought, searching the water for the boat he heard. *How long does stealth take?*

Finally, he spotted the boat, coming straight toward him at the abandoned marina on the outskirts of Naples.

It was them. He recognized the man leaning away from the tubing that held the roof on. The boat continued up the wide creek mouth, moving quickly, until just before the rickety dock on which Manish was standing.

He didn't react or panic, and the boat slowed suddenly, turned, then came up against the dock fairly hard.

Damien jumped out and approached Manish very closely, standing over him in a threatening way. "You said it'd be guarded by two *men*," he snarled, eyes flashing with anger. "You did *not* say they'd be two fucking *cops*."

"What difference does it make? Did you find the gold?"

Damien's broad shoulders sank slightly, but he remained highly agitated. "No gold. We killed two cops, boarded the sub, and searched everywhere."

"The torpedo tubes?" Manish asked. "Were they welded shut?"

"First place we looked," he replied. "Both forward tubes had been welded, just like you said. But they were cut open recently with an angle grinder. Whoever it was, they left their tools."

CHAPTER THIRTY

It wasn't that I didn't trust this new cousin of Rusty's. I'd only just met the guy, and because of that, I had no reason to distrust him, either.

It was just that the *timing* was suspect.

We knew someone had likely been tracking Herman's internet searches, probably flagging certain keywords on the internet. Could those same people send in a quiet, unassuming operative posing as a retired accountant to gain information?

Keep your friends close, and your enemies closer.

The only reaction Hoyt had to my declaration about the murders was one of surprise and revulsion. I could read it in his micro expressions. Though he was a big man, he appeared to be non-violent.

"That's terrible!" he exclaimed. "Did you know the men who were killed?"

"They work for Jesse's daughter, Kim," Rusty admitted. "She and her husband are lieutenants with the Florida Fish and Wildlife Conservation Commission—the state's water cops."

"Rusty and I only met the two men twice," I said. "That's why we have to fly up there. We were probably the last ones to see them alive yesterday evening."

"It's no problem," Hoyt said. "I need to get a room anyway. What's the best hotel in town?"

"Casa Thurman," Rusty proclaimed. "You'll stay with us; we got three extra rooms and Rufus serves three meals a day. No arguin'."

He smiled broadly. "In that case, cousin, I accept."

"No tellin' how long we'll be gone," Rusty said. "But my wife should be home any minute. In the meantime, you can hang out with some cool locals and explore the property."

"You could charge a fee for the drive in from the highway," Hoyt said. "Is it always so lush?"

"A number of volunteers help maintain it," I replied. "And I've been telling Rusty that for years."

"Is there any chance I can go with you?" Hoyt asked. "I've never seen the Everglades, and a boat salvage operation sounds interesting, minus the two deceased officers, that is. I assume that's what you're waiting for? Removal of the bodies?"

I raised an eyebrow. "How'd you come to that conclusion?"

Thirty-three million in gold would bring all kinds of slithering creatures out from under rocks. My gut told me Hoyt was a decent person, but I'd been wrong before. At any rate, if he were with *us*, he wouldn't become a threat.

"I'm afraid I watch too many late-night true-crime shows," he continued. "I wouldn't want to actually *see* anything like that, of course, but salvaging an old boat interests me greatly."

I laughed inwardly. You could take a Thurman away from the sea, but you couldn't remove the sea from a Thurman. Rusty's lineage included a number of New England's finest sea captains.

Also, Rusty had always said it was *Sid* who liked to watch those forensics and true-crime shows. But I knew it was Rusty.

It was interesting to see the similarities in the two men.

"I'll have to clear it with Kim first," I replied. "She's supposed to call just about—"

Suddenly my phone chirped and vibrated in my pocket. It was Kim, so I answered it immediately and without preamble.

"We're at the Rusty Anchor," I told her, "and can be wheels up in twenty minutes. On site in under an hour."

"The ME is leaving now," Kim said. "Forensics will be here for a while longer. What's with the solar panels?"

"I'll explain it all when we get there," I said. "And I'll call Billy now and get him moving. Okay to bring a fourth? Rusty's cousin?"

"Maddy? Why on earth would she be coming?"

"Not Maddy," I replied. "A different cousin. A guy named Hoyt. He just arrived in town this morning."

Kim was intuitive and she knew I was often involved with people who at first seemed unconnected. She would likely assume that if I wanted him there, it was for a reason.

"He stays in the plane or on the aft deck of the sub," she replied, then the call went dead.

"You can come," I relayed to Hoyt, as I pulled Billy's number up on the screen. "You'll have to restrict your movement, though. Forensics people are still there."

"*What* will you explain when we get there?" Rusty asked.

"The answer to her first question," I replied. "The solar panels."

Some color leached out of Rusty's face.

"Don't worry," I told him. "We were doing everything by the book."

"Am I… missing something?" Hoyt asked.

I considered myself a better-than-average judge of character, though that notion *had* bitten me in the ass a time or three. But Hoyt was *Rusty's* family, not mine, and the salvage operation was also his.

"You want to tell him what you're salvaging?" I asked my old friend.

Hoyt looked from me to Rusty. "What is it?"

"It's an eighty-year-old Nazi submarine," Rusty revealed. "I been dyin' to tell someone outside of our little circle for two years."

"You've got to be..." Hoyt stammered, eyes bugging in complete, unveiled surprise. "Seriously? A submarine? But you said it was in the Everglades."

"It was driven deep into the Glades by the Cuba-Florida Hurricane of 1944," Rusty explained. "More'n ten miles deep."

Hoyt's eyes went wide once more. "My birth mother's dad was killed in that storm, and she nearly was."

"We'd better get going," I said, figuring Rusty would tell him about the gold eventually. "You were adopted locally?"

"Not down here," Hoyt replied, as they followed me out the door. "I was born in Naples and adopted privately there, through a local doctor. My adoptive parents moved out west when I was six."

"You weren't born in Colorado?" I asked, then realized instantly that his birth mother, if she'd been unmarried, had probably been discharged when her pregnancy became obvious, and she would have returned home.

"Jesse's from Fort Myers," Rusty said, closing the door, then locking it. "I used to visit his place there when his Mam and Pap were still alive."

"We used to visit Fort Myers Beach every summer when I was little," Hoyt said. "I don't remember much, except that I liked being there. You two go back a long time, then?"

"Met on the bus to Parris Island," Rusty replied. "Marine Corps boot camp. We weren't no more'n kids and been best buds ever since."

"We can take my car," Hoyt offered, as he noticed we were heading toward the three apparent derelict vehicles under the oak tree.

I clicked the buttons on my key fob and *The Beast's* diesel engine started right up. "No need. They know mine at the airport gate."

"Will it make it that far?" Hoyt asked in a joking tone as he opened the back door. "Oh, wow! Nice interior."

"The looks prevent theft," I said, getting in the front seat as Rusty went around the hood. "*Outside*, it's a fifty-two-year-old beater. But everything inside and what makes it go are just getting broken in. But I don't drive very often."

Sid's car came into the lot just as I was about to pull out from under the tree, and Rusty stopped me. "Give me just a sec to tell her we're leavin'."

Although it was obvious we were leaving, and Sid had known we were going to be, I backed under the oak again after Rusty got out and trotted over to Sid's car as she was getting out.

"She's quite tall," Hoyt said from the backseat.

"She's six-three in those heels," I said as three young people passed in front of us, all with blond hair. "Rusty's only five-six."

The young woman in the trio looked at us through the windshield, or rather, she looked at me. For just enough too long to ping the reptilian part of my brain.

She smiled.

Some call it instinct, or a sixth sense, but it's really just the fight-or-flight conditioning of thousands of years of evolution, when trouble is either apparent or perceived.

I studied the sides of the two young men's faces, committing all three to memory as they continued toward the door of the restaurant.

It wasn't unusual for people to look at *The Beast* when she was running. Most, like Hoyt, figured she wouldn't. *The Beast* looked like a piece of crap, except for her oversized tires and wheels. But the big diesel engine chugging beneath the hood indicated something else.

The woman was young, probably early twenties, tall, slim, blue-eyed, with a very pale complexion. And she was absolutely drop-dead gorgeous.

She said something to the two men as they reached the door, and they both looked back toward me for a second before disappearing inside.

The two men were older, but not by much, and like the girl, very pale. Obviously newcomers or tourists, and if I had to guess, they were probably related.

CHAPTER THIRTY-ONE

Just over an hour later, we landed on Whitewater Bay for the second time in less than a day. I idled *Island Hopper* toward the submarine, over near the northeast shore.

There were four other boats tied up to it, all on the starboard side, where the sub was tethered to the mooring balls.

That left me with no choice but to tie up to the port side again.

"Same as before?" Rusty asked, as I angled toward the aft part of the sub.

"There's Marty," I said, spotting my son-in-law moving toward the stern. "I'll try to get us closer this time."

"I'm not believing what I'm seeing," Hoyt said over the intercom from the backseat. "But we only flew over the coast a couple of miles back. You said it'd been driven more than *ten* miles into the Everglades."

"It was," Rusty said, looking back at him for a second. "We moved it recently and we're waiting here for the last of the channels to be dredged and a lock built."

"Get ready," I said, reaching for the switch to turn on the magnetos.

"If you're waitin' on me, you're backin' up," Rusty said as he opened the door and then climbed out, moving to the aft storage locker on the float to get the dock line.

Hoyt watched him, obviously enjoying the adventure he was witnessing, even with the shadow of death hanging over it.

This time, I waited until we were a little closer before I killed the engine and stepped on the left rudder pedal.

Marty ducked under the wing and Rusty was able to reach up and hand him the dock line before fending the plane's float away from the sub.

Rusty and Marty tied *Island Hopper* off quickly while I went through the post-flight procedure.

Hoyt and I were both going to have to climb over Rusty's seat to exit the plane. I'd done it many times, but I was worried about Hoyt.

I needn't have been concerned, though. The Beaver's cockpit was roomy for most people but I'm six-three, so getting my *legs* in and out was the hardest part.

Once I was up on the sub's deck, Hoyt climbed out quite easily, then came up the ladder to the deck beside us.

"Marty," I said, as Kim approached, "This is Hoyt Cooper, Rusty's cousin. He just arrived from out of town this morning to meet Rusty for the first time."

"I was adopted at birth," Hoyt explained, sticking his hand out.

"And this is my daughter, Kim," I added.

They both shook his hand, then I turned toward Kim. "There's something you don't know."

She looked up, meeting my gaze. "There was something of value on this submarine. It was hidden in the forward torpedo tubes. I remember you mentioning once that they'd been welded shut for some reason, and that's no longer the case."

The roar of an engine could be heard just to the east, and when I looked, I saw Billy's airboat turning around a cypress head hard on the starboard chine as it accelerated across the water toward us.

I glanced at Rusty, then Hoyt. "Let's go forward and help Billy tie off."

Rusty understood why, and I could see Kim figuring it out, as well.

She turned to Hoyt and said, "You'll have to wait here by the plane, Mr. Cooper. This is still a crime scene."

Rusty and I followed Marty and Kim forward. There wasn't anyone else in sight, but the other three boats indicated someone was *inside* the sub. Several someones.

Billy spotted us moving past the conning tower, and I motioned him to come alongside just in front of the Monroe County forensics boat.

He slowed and soon came up alongside, killing the engine. His platform up on top was the same height as the sub's deck, but a good three feet away. Billy had no trouble leaping across, a single bow line in hand.

I glanced back at Hoyt. "I didn't want to explain this in front of Rusty's cousin. We only just met." I turned and faced Kim. "You were right. The attackers thought there was something of great value aboard the sub."

"Was?" she asked.

"I found it yesterday," Billy said. "While I was here working."

"What was it?" Marty asked him.

"There were twenty-four gold bars hidden in the torpedo tubes," Billy replied, the relief apparent in his voice. "Each is marked 400-troy ounces of Swiss gold."

"That's over six hundred pounds!" Marty whisper-shouted. "Where is it now?"

"Stashed in my hangar at the airport," I replied. "With Chyrel watching over it."

"And those solar panels?" Kim asked. "How is that connected?"

Rusty actually looked down at his feet. "It was my idea," he admitted. "We'd just finished loadin' the gold in the plane when your guys showed up, so I made out like that was the reason we was here all day."

She looked from Rusty to me, then back at him again. "Two of my men are dead, Uncle Rusty," she said, quietly but firmly. "Had they known, they might have been more alert to danger. When did you know about this gold?"

"When I cut the welds yesterday and found it," Billy replied. "I called your father right away. He was leaving Key West with Rusty, and they flew up here as soon as they could."

Kim looked up at me. "Do you know who it was, Dad?"

I returned her gaze for a second, then looked out over the bay toward the creek inlet, remembering the first attack.

"No, I don't," I replied. "And that bothers me."

CHAPTER THIRTY-TWO

A uniformed Monroe County deputy climbed up the ladder to the conning tower's observation deck, turned and looked back down, then bent and retrieved an orange box from someone below.

A moment later, a woman's blond hair appeared, then she climbed out and turned forward, seeing us on the bow. It was Detective Sergeant Diane Pine.

She quickly descended to the deck and strode toward us, her eyes fixed on mine. "I might have known you'd be involved."

"You two know each other?" Kim asked.

Pine looked at Kim as if seeing her for the first time, and I caught her eyes moving down to the silver bars on Kim's uniform collar and her name tag, pinned to her blouse.

"I was the primary case agent on a murder investigation in Marathon last summer, Lieutenant Philips," Pine replied. "One of Mr. McDermitt's employees took a bullet meant for him."

She was acting a bit aggressive, and my only thought was that she was attempting to cover up the fact that I'd recruited her as an Armstrong informant.

"Gregor Albert," Kim said. "I know all about it."

"With all due respect, Lieutenant," Pine said, "that's doubtful."

Kim smiled at her, like a cat ready to pounce. "Probably more than *you* know about it, Detective. Mr. McDermitt is my father and Gregor was a long-time family friend."

Pine's poker face hadn't gotten any better.

She glanced around at the others, recognizing Rusty and Billy before her eyes settled on Marty. "And you?"

"Lieutenant *Martin* Philips," he replied. "And I'm Mr. McDermitt's son-in-law."

She looked around at them again. "Daughter, son-in-law, and two best friends." Then she jerked a thumb toward the stern where Hoyt was watching what was going on. "And who's he? A long-lost cousin?"

It couldn't be helped, and may have relieved some tension, as first Rusty, then me, and even Kim began laughing. Billy and Marty just looked at one another.

"As a matter of fact, Diane," I said. "That's exactly who Hoyt is. A cousin Rusty recently connected with, and who he never knew about." I had a feeling as to why she was playing all hard-ass, and added, "He doesn't know *anything* about Armstrong, but the rest do."

Her face showed relief. "That's good. I didn't know what to say when I saw you here."

"You know each other through Armstrong Research?" Kim asked.

"Not exactly," I replied. "Savvy and I recruited Diane as an independent informant."

Kim turned to face the slightly younger detective. "Have you met any of the people?"

Pine looked from her to me, then back again, before replying. "Just your mother and father, plus an older man who approached me, just last week."

"Savannah's my *step*mother," Kim replied. "An *older* man?"

"It was weird," she replied. "He sat down on the sand next to me at the beach last week. At first, I just thought he was another trolling tourist, but then he calmly started telling me things nobody should know; things about me, about some of my cases..." She paused and faced me. "Even my family and my past."

"A tall, gray-haired man with a crew cut?" I asked. "Built like a Sherman tank with skin like tanned leather, and talks like a three-pack-a-day Camel smoker?"

She nodded. "Who was he?"

"Stockwell." Kim and I said in unison.

"As he stood up to leave, he said he was from Armstrong," Pine replied. "But he never gave a name." She turned toward me again. "In fact, the only name he mentioned was yours."

"Travis Stockwell," I began. "Former Army colonel, Ranger, Special Forces, former Homeland Security deputy director, all-around badass, and now the head of security for Armstrong Research's Mobile Expeditionary Division—ARMED."

"He never asked me anything," Pine said. "And when I asked how he knew those things, he just walked away. You're not kidding about a tank; four young guys moved wide around him. What the hell was that all about?"

I grinned at her. "You've never been interviewed for a promotion?"

She stared at me for a brief moment, then turned back to Kim.

"Forensics is almost finished," Diane said. "They'll be leaving shortly, and two of my guys will be staying." Then she turned to Rusty. "The sheriff wants this thing out of here as soon as possible."

Rusty held both hands up, palms out. "I'm just the salvage operator on record. If they'd contracted *me* to dig the channel, this thing'd be in Key West already, runnin' like a top, and conductin' sunset tours. Tell Rick to call DNR. That's who's draggin' their flip-flops."

She turned back to Kim. "At any rate, I'll see that you get the full report, but to cut to the chase, they didn't find anything. The only prints they came up with came from your father and his two friends here, courtesy of Uncle Sam."

"They wore gloves," I said. "Professionals. What about ballistics? anything traceable?"

"We'll know more after the autopsy," Pine said. "But both officers had multiple gunshot wounds to the torso, with few exit wounds. My guess is they used handguns, no more than forty-caliber."

"Tight grouping," I said. "How could they have gotten so close to here without being spotted or at least heard? Out here at night, you can hear a gator take a breath half a mile away."

"The bigger question," Pine said, glancing back toward where the forensics people were loading one of the boats. "How did they even know where 'here' is?"

CHAPTER THIRTY-THREE

There were two unasked questions hanging in the air like the scent of ozone from an approaching electrical storm just before its fury is unleashed.

Though Kim *was* my daughter, she was also a law-enforcement officer, and she hadn't asked anything more about the gold besides where it was currently located. Being my daughter, she knew that whatever our plans were for the gold, it wouldn't be anything illicit or immoral.

Pine knew my connection to Armstrong, but didn't really know me, nor did she know about the gold.

"Those tools up in the front part?" Pine finally asked. "And what looks like recent grinding work on the doors of the torpedo tubes? Was something hidden in there? Something someone was willing to *kill* for?"

"Long story short," Rusty said. "This sub, the U-320, was reported sunk in the North Sea. But her captain limped into a port where it became part of the 'rat lines' out of Germany toward the end of the war, and a bunch of high-rankin' Nazi officers had a fortune in gold stashed in them tubes."

"Gold?" she asked, her tone flat. "Where did it come from?"

Rusty pulled several pages of folded paper from his pocket—the notes from Herman—then explained everything they'd learned so far, the number of surviving descendants of the Dutch Jews who were robbed and nearly exterminated, who the German officers were, and what their roles were in the occupation of Amsterdam, as well as who was in charge of the operation. He ended it with the fact that he was very close to brokering a deal to return the gold to Amsterdam.

"Where is it now?" Pine asked. "Although it wasn't *here* when the shootings took place, it will still need to be catalogued and processed as material evidence."

"Evi—" Rusty stammered. "It was taken from those folks more'n eighty years ago!" He stabbed a finger at the names on the page. "These men were responsible for loadin' the last boxcars to Auschwitz!"

"It can't be helped," Pine said. "After that long, what's a few more days?" She glanced at Kim. "Right, Lieutenant?"

Kim nodded, turning to Rusty. "It *is* prima facie evidence, Uncle Rusty. It might take a few days, or several weeks. But all your licenses and permits are in order. The gold was discovered on this sub, which you're currently salvaging, so it belongs to you."

"From a legal standpoint, maybe," Rusty countered. "But from a moral view, it don't."

"How many people does your plane hold?" Pine asked me.

"Six," I replied, understanding the reason for the question.

"I'll fly back with you," she said. "We can have a patrol deputy meet us at the airport to take the gold to the substation for safe keeping."

"I think you might want to have them bring something larger," I said. "Like a Brink's truck with a few extra armed guards."

Her eyes widened. "How much gold are we talking?"

"Six hundred and seventy pound*s*," Billy replied. "Give or take a troy ounce or two."

She glanced at him questioningly, then back at me.

I nodded. "About thirty-three million dollars at today's price. It's safe in my hangar, Diane. *Chyrel* is watching it."

"Chyrel is…" her voice trailed off. "Thirty-three million…"

She looked back at the conning tower. "They were war criminals?"

"*War* criminals?" Marty echoed.

"That's where it appears Rusty and Herman's research is pointing," I said. "Germans have always kept meticulous records. Herman figured out that the names recorded in the captain's logbook had all been men who'd commanded various units of the occupation forces in Amsterdam, *and* they were responsible for the dismantling of Jewish-owned businesses, banks, communities, homes, lives, and the extermination of tens of thousands."

"War crimes," Kim said softly. She turned and looked at me, then Billy and Rusty in turn. "Of course it would be you three who'd uncover it."

Pine took her phone out and looked at the screen. "No signal. I'll use one of the boat's radios and arrange for a SWAT van to meet us at the airport."

I put a hand on her arm as she started to turn. "How about waiting until we're close enough for a cell call? A radio isn't very secure."

She nodded in agreement. "Nor is our dispatch system," she reminded me. "And probably not our phones."

"I have a burn phone on the plane," I offered. "Never used. Do you know someone you trust who you can call to get things moving by word of mouth?"

"Good idea," she agreed, then jerked a thumb aft. "What about cousin Hoyt?"

"He don't know nothin' about any of this," Rusty said. "We met through that Ancestry DNA thing and set up a meet and greet for this mornin'. Planned it all yesterday, before any of this happened."

"I get the feeling he's trustworthy," I said. "Rusty should tell him what's going on. He might feel uneasy about riding back with us, knowing two men have already died for what we're going back to get."

"It would certainly make conversation in the airplane a lot easier," Pine added.

"Want I should tell him now?" Rusty asked.

I nodded, and he turned and started back toward the plane, where Hoyt was waiting.

"That's the last of the forensics people," Pine said, as a third man carrying an orange case climbed into one of the boats and the outboard started. "I'll have Deputy Gordon take our boat back without me." She turned to Kim. "The other boat and two deputies will remain on scene with your two men, and I'll arrange to have around-the-clock watches to supplement yours. What's your rotation schedule?"

"The first shift is midnight to six," Kim replied. "Relief every six hours."

"I'll set up the same six-hour watches," Pine offered. "But send out reliefs at three and nine, so we have fresh eyes and ears every three hours."

"Thanks," Marty said. "It's very troubling that they were able to get so close undetected. Mahoney and Sinclair were good officers."

The last of Kim's and Diane's people were off the sub. Kim had relieved the two officers who'd found the bodies and sent them home as soon as she and Marty had secured the crime scene and gotten their statements. *Their* relief had gotten to the sub just before we had.

The two FWC officers, sitting in their boat, scowled openly at us as we started toward the plane.

"I brought a spare lock," Billy said, pulling one from a pocket. "Is it all right if I lock things up now?"

Pine shook her head. "They didn't cut the lock off, Mr. Rainwater; they cut the steel hasp."

"Why would they do that?" Billy complained. "I leave my truck unlocked for just that reason. It's easier for a thief to find out that I don't keep anything valuable in it. And what happens? Some ass... *person* busted out my window anyway."

"It would've been a lot easier," she agreed. "It looks like they used an angle grinder, probably battery-powered, to cut the two-inch weld rather than the quarter-inch lock. Which brings up a question."

"How did they know to bring one?" Kim said. "Not something a bunch of 'good 'ol boys' on airboats carry around." She paused and looked forward to the conning tower. "I don't think the men who came out here and killed my officers are all that are involved. This has the earmarks of an organized effort."

My mind went back more than two years. "A very *patient* organization; this wasn't the first time."

CHAPTER THIRTY-FOUR

Kim, of course, already knew what had happened more than two years earlier, as well as the shooting at the Rusty Anchor. With time being of the essence, I told Pine that I'd explain it to her once we were airborne.

We said our goodbyes, got in the plane, and within minutes, we were in the air. Once I leveled off, I turned due south, then asked Hoyt to unplug his headset for a few minutes. He did so, without question, but left it still on to reduce the engine noise.

Rusty had told him about the gold, but what I was about to explain to Detective Sergeant Diane Pine could put both me and Rusty behind bars.

Diane was sitting up front with me and I glanced over at her as I started to explain what had happened two years ago when we'd found the sub. I told her of my suspicions at the time, and what they were now.

"We found out later who they were, but not much else," I concluded. "Three grandsons and a granddaughter of the sub's captain."

"And they fired on you first?" she asked.

"Four rounds," Rusty and I replied in unison. "And one almost hit me," he added.

"Why didn't you report it?" she asked in her cop voice.

I looked over at her. "Chyrel found out later that two of them were in the country illegally," I said. "And the other two had gone to Cuba, then reentered the U.S. illegally. To report the attack, we'd have had to report the find, and we weren't ready to do that. I was fired on by unknown assailants and returned fire. What was there to report?"

By mentioning Chyrel, who Pine was familiar with, I hoped to convey without saying it that Armstrong Research was involved.

"What else do you know about the four grandchildren?" she asked.

"Karl and Lucas Crittenden," I replied. "They were the sons of Hans Crittenden, Jr., whose father was captain of the U-320. Their second cousins, Hannah Hoffman and Paul Schmidt were in on it too."

"Paul Schmidt, Paul Schmidt," Diane repeated. "Where do I know that name?"

"He was shot and killed a few days before the attack," I replied. "At the Rusty Anchor."

She turned in her seat to look back at Rusty. "Are there a lot of shootings at your place?"

"Not usually," Rusty replied, then grinned. "Everyone knows I keep a deck sweeper behind the bar."

"A deck sweeper?"

"Sawed-off twelve-gauge pump," he replied.

"I don't know how much of this I can overlook," Diane said, turning back in her seat. "Armstrong or not. Did that Stockwell guy know what happened two years ago?"

"He did," I replied.

"I still don't know what I can just forget I've heard," she grumbled.

"All of it," I replied. "Everything I just told you never happened."

"Yes, well, I don't think I can—"

"Yes," I said, cutting her off. "You can and you *will*. Do you remember your answer when I asked you if you'd pull the trigger?"

"This is different," she said. "You're asking me to overlook multiple murders."

"I'm not asking, Diane," I replied. "I'm telling. And self-defense isn't murder."

She was quiet for a moment. "You said Stockwell knew about it? Was it like an assignment or something?"

I shook my head. "No, but once assets were threatened, Armstrong helped out immensely. I sometimes think there's not an altercation in the world that Stockwell doesn't know about."

"I'll sit on this for now," she said, reluctance in her tone. "Do you know anything more about those four grandchildren, Karl and Lucas, you said... and?"

"Hannah Hoffman and Paul Schmidt," I replied. "I'd bet my last nickel that *they* weren't pulling the strings either. I had the suspicion then that someone else was directing their movements. Someone with pretty unlimited technical ability."

"How old were they?" she asked. "Any idea?"

"Oh, he'll have more than an *idea*," Rusty said from the back.

"The two brothers would be forty-three and thirty-two now," I replied. "Karl was the oldest. The cousins were closer to Lucas's age."

Simultaneously, two images popped into my head—the passport photo of Hannah Hoffman, and the girl I'd seen entering the Rusty Anchor as we were leaving.

At least a decade apart in age, maybe two, but very similar in appearance.

"Check your phone," I told Diane. "If you have a signal, make your call and tell your friend *two* things." I paused and glanced in the mirror at Rusty. "Tell him to roll the SWAT van to the airport and to also send a deputy to the Rusty Anchor."

"What's goin' on, bro?" Rusty asked urgently.

"You probably didn't see them," I said, looking in the mirror. "You were talking to Sid just before we left, but two young men and a young woman were going in, and the woman looked almost exactly like Hannah Hoffman."

"But you said they were in their late thirties or forties," Diane said, checking her phone. "Still no signal."

"I know we're old, bro," Rusty said, "but forties ain't exactly young."

"It wasn't Hoffman," I replied. "She's definitely dead, but all three of those young people I saw as we were leaving were blond, blue-eyed, and very pale."

"Just like them that came shootin' at the Anchor," Rusty said. "I remember seein' the pictures you guys found."

"Do you think those three might somehow be related to what happened two years ago?" Diane asked. "I mean, besides profiling them as members of the Aryan Nation."

"Just a gut feeling," I replied. "But something like that. Maybe they were the offspring of one of the captain's grandchildren?"

"I have a signal," Diane said. "What should I tell him to look for or ask for when he gets there?"

I thought about it for a moment. If they *were* dangerous and for whatever reason decided to take over the Anchor, the only resistance they'd have met would've been Dink and John. But what if they were armed?

"Tell him to play it cool," I said. "Tell him to just walk up to the bar and ask if Shorty's been in today."

"Who's he?"

"My dad," Rusty replied. "Good idea, bro. Everyone knew or heard of Pop."

"If anyone says anything other than he's been dead for thirty years," I replied, "then something's wrong and he should go back out to the highway and wait for backup,"

Rusty sat forward in his seat. "You don't think—"

"I'm not thinking anything," I said. "But considering what's happened, what's at stake, and what all we *don't* know, I think it'd pay to be cautious."

Diane made her call, and to her credit, she sounded professional and organized in what she wanted done, by whom, and how the orders were to be relayed.

"Call me back the minute you leave the Rusty Anchor," she concluded, then ended the call.

I told Rusty to have Hoyt plug his headset back in, and I was impressed that he didn't ask a bunch of questions. Perhaps his accounting background made him less nosey.

When I contacted Miami Center to get wind and weather, they gave me a different weather report than the usual canned message.

Winds were now northwesterly but very light, so I could enter the pattern from the west with a slight tail wind or circle around. When I made the call on the unicom frequency of my intent to land I heard no response.

The west end of the Seven Mile Bridge lay just ahead, and I started a slow turn to fly parallel with it, about a half mile away. Even with a tail wind, I'd need less than half the runway.

Nearing the high bridge arch, I pointed the nose down and we slowly descended. I added flaps when we were a mile from the runway's threshold and reduced power, so we were barely passing the north-bound traffic on the bridge.

As I lowered the landing gear, Diane's phone rang, and she tapped the screen before putting the phone under her headset.

"Pine," she said, then listened for a moment. She turned to me and said, "The bartender said Shorty left an hour ago."

"Get him out!" I said urgently, reaching up and going to full takeoff power. "And get backup in there now!"

CHAPTER THIRTY-FIVE

Rusty's parents, Shorty and Dreama, had run the bar for decades before Rusty took over. Back then, it'd been a dive bar and bait shop, but just like everyone in the Keys now knew Rusty, they all knew Shorty, and back then, nearly every angler who wet a line got bait from him.

Something was wrong at the Rusty Anchor, and I suspected those three blond kids I'd seen were right in the middle of it.

I had an idea. It was risky, but a bunch of cops rolling into the Rusty Anchor parking lot could be far worse. Those three kids, which was what they were, probably assumed there was only one way into Rusty's property, and if they felt cornered, anything could happen.

When I reached down and retracted the landing gear, then reduced the flaps, Diane turned toward me in surprise.

"What are you doing?" she asked urgently. "We need to get this plane down, now!"

Banking right, I flew *Island Hopper* out over the bridge, just off Sunset Key, giving the tourists who were starting to gather a bit of a show.

Several people waved.

"There's definitely something wrong at the Anchor," I explained to her, continuing my turn. "Your guys are going to need a diversion. Tell your people to get set up in the driveway, ready to move in on foot when they hear us coming up the ramp."

I leveled off, heading west-southwest, toward Party Island.

"What ramp?" she asked, frustration evident in her voice. "Where?"

"The boat ramp at the rear of Rusty's property," I said. "If your guys go charging in there right after they've been visited by a cop, anything could happen. We'll land in the water and make a lot of noise going up the ramp. Trust me, they'll hear this engine, and they'll be looking *away* from the driveway."

She got on the phone again, relaying my plan and coordinating with two people at once, it sounded like.

When I reached the other side of the Seven Mile Bridge, I banked left, out to sea, and continued around until I was again parallel with the long bridge, but this time to the south of it, and headed back toward Marathon.

"Don't move until you hear the sound of the airplane coming up the ramp," Pine said, then pulled her phone down and turned to me. "They parked on the highway and are spread out on both sides of the driveway."

"How many?"

"Six deputies on scene now," she replied. "Two more nearly there, and SWAT is five minutes out. All rolling silent."

I grinned, thinking what Russ had pounded into our heads, and Pap and even my dad had taught me all my life. When somebody hits you, hit them back *harder* and with everything you had, to take away any will they might have to continue the fight. It worked in the playgrounds of Fort Myers just as well as on the battlefield in the desert.

When overwhelmed with superior numbers and firepower, the

fight- or-flight response in most people will be instantly turned off, usually replaced with docile resignation.

The risky part was for us and *Island Hopper*.

A floatplane waddling up out of the water might not be all that uncommon around South Florida, but if those three were from where I thought they were, they'd likely never even seen one before and might not feel that sense of overwhelming force when observing *Island Hopper's* ungainliness on land. They might simply open fire on us.

I lowered the flaps again as we flew past Sister Rock, off the southern tip of Key Vaca and the town of Marathon. Checking the landing gear, I had four blue lights, indicating the landing gear was up and locked for a water landing.

We all craned our necks to look toward the Rusty Anchor, just to the north, but we were too far away to see much of anything.

There weren't any boats on the water where we'd be landing, and after a moment, I banked left, just off of Key Colony Beach, and reduced power.

I lined the nose up with the actual wind direction, heading straight toward Rusty's ramp.

"Get ready," Diane said. "We're descending."

"Tell them not to go when they hear the engine out here on the water," I warned. "When we go up the ramp, I'll make sure the roar is unmistakable."

She relayed my warning just as the floats made contact with the water and we slowed quickly. I added a little power to keep the floats up on the steps and gently turned toward a spot fifty feet out from the ramp.

I couldn't see anyone out in the large yard between the restaurant and the rum shack.

When we were a hundred yards away from the deep end of the ramp, I throttled back and let the floats settle into the water.

Still fifty yards out, I lowered the landing gear and got four green lights. There was a little bit of crosswind, pushing us to the left, which I easily countered with a little right pedal to turn the floats' rudders.

The nose gear made contact with the submerged ramp, and I added just a little throttle until I felt the main gear touch. Then I applied light pressure on the brake and throttled up to takeoff power.

The big radial engine roared in mighty defiance, shaking the plane with a buffeting propwash that created some lift over the wings.

I eased the brakes just enough to let *Island Hopper* climb slowly up out of the water at full power, then waddle slowly up the ramp.

I didn't throttle back until we reached the top of the ramp and I saw nearly a dozen men in black tactical garb sprinting toward the front door of the restaurant, pistol and rifle barrels leading the way.

Suddenly, the back door of the restaurant burst open. A man rushed outside to the deck rail. It was one of the two young men I'd seen earlier.

He stood defiantly at the rail and raised a pistol.

My instinct took control as I stomped on the left rudder pedal, released the brakes, and revved the engine for a second.

The sudden propwash on *Island Hopper's* control surfaces pivoted the tail around sharply, turning away from the threat.

As I killed the engine and locked the brakes up, Diane pushed her hatch open even before the plane stopped rocking.

She drew her sidearm with her left hand, extending both hands through the gap between the hatch and the frame.

"Monroe County Sheriff's deputy!" Diane shouted over the sudden silence. "Drop your weapon!"

The kid on the deck didn't comply and started shooting wildly. I heard a popping sound toward the back of the plane.

Diane fired twice, and the man's body jerked with each shot before he fell down the steps to the ground.

Even from more than a hundred feet away, I could tell he was dead before he fell down the steps.

I looked over at Pine with new respect. A hundred feet is a long shot with a handgun.

CHAPTER THIRTY-SIX

The whole thing was over in a matter of seconds. Diane had us wait in the plane until she got word from her partner that the scene was secure and there was only one minor injury. Then we all climbed out and ran for the rear deck.

I paused with Diane as she knelt beside the man she'd shot and checked for a pulse.

I didn't need to check, looking down into the lifeless blue eyes of one of the men I'd seen entering the Rusty Anchor. It was obvious he was dead.

Diane rose slowly, and I touched her shoulder. "There was nothing you could have done."

The back door opened and a tall man in a black Monroe County Sheriff's windbreaker stepped out, stopping Rusty and Hoyt from entering.

Diane looked up at me, and I could not just *see* the torment in her eyes, I could feel it. "He's just a kid. Why'd he have to do that?"

"This won't be easy to process for a while, Diane," I told her. "But each of us *chooses* our own path in life, and all too often, bad choices lead to something like this. He opened fire first."

"You okay, Diane?" the black-clad man called from the deck.

She turned, and we started toward the steps. "Yeah, Bruce, I'm all right. One perp shot and killed. Anyone hurt inside?"

"One guy shot in the leg," the man replied. I noticed he wore sergeant chevrons on his collar. "He'll be okay, though."

"These three are with me," Diane said, then nodded at Rusty. "He's the owner. They can go in."

He stepped aside, and Rusty rushed through the door.

"You know the drill, Diane," the other sergeant said. "Have a seat out here. The chaplain's on his—"

"I don't need a chaplain!" she snapped.

"I know," he said, his voice soft. "But it's protocol. Want me to sit out here with you?"

"I'll be okay, Bruce," she replied with a sigh. "Who else is here?"

Bruce pressed the button on the mic clipped to the collar of his tactical vest. "Unit four, unit two, tac three."

With his left hand, the sergeant changed the channel on the radio secured to his belt. "Unit four?" He paused, listening through a wired earbud. "Come out back, Charlie. Diane's been in an OIS and I'm separating her."

Bruce turned to me. "You can go inside, Mr. McDermitt."

My eyes were on Diane. "Are you going to be okay?"

She nodded. "Standard procedure. I'm no longer involved in the investigation but will now be the *subject* of one. Go inside, Jesse. Check on your people."

I reached out and gripped her shoulder with one hand, and when she looked into my eyes, I said, "They're your people too, Diane. I've been where you are now. You have my number."

She nodded. "I'll be—"

"No. You won't," I said gently. "Maybe right now. And maybe in a few days. But tonight's going to be rough. Do you have someone?"

"We've got it, Mr. McDermitt," Bruce said. "Please go inside. I'll be in to take your statement in a moment."

When I entered through the back door, I saw four deputies escorting the young woman I'd seen with the two men out the front door, her hands cuffed behind her back. Outside, the young man was similarly cuffed and being put into a squad car.

Looking around, the first person I noticed was Larry, sitting in a chair near the front door, a bloody bar rag tied around his leg a few inches above the knee. He motioned quickly for me, and I went straight over.

"Hiya, Jesse," Larry said, smiling, though I could tell he was in pain. "I want you to meet someone."

A small boy sat in a chair beside Larry, his feet drawn up on the chair, and his arms around his knees. He looked eight or nine, but if the kid was who I thought he was, he'd have to be at least eleven.

"Mason," Larry said to the boy, "this is the man I've been telling you about, Jesse McDermitt." Larry looked up at me. "Jesse, this is my friend from school, Mason Slate."

I squatted down to eye level and stuck my hand out. "Hey, Mason. That's a cool name. Can we trade?"

His eyes flitted to mine for a second, then he looked back down as he extended a small hand.

I shook it. "Did you see what happened, Mason?"

Again, his eyes came up and met mine, but only for a fraction of a second longer, and he nodded.

An EMT came through the door and rushed toward us. Larry fixed the man with a hard stare and held up a hand, palm out. "Give us a minute, please."

"Sir, you're blee—"

Larry's eyes flashed and his brow furrowed. Then he relaxed his expression. "I know I am," he said calmly, but with the same intense gaze. "Give us a minute, please."

The paramedic backed off, and Larry turned to the boy. "If they have to take me to the hospital," he said, "I want you to stay here with Jesse until Ms. Lauren or Ms. Chyrel arrive." Larry looked up at me and added, "Rusty said he called Savvy before you landed. She and Lauren are on the way."

That would mean that Alberto and Tank would be coming also, which, given the scene, might be beneficial.

"Mason was standing next to me," Larry said, gritting his teeth slightly. "It was the *girl* who shot me. She was aiming right at my chest."

I heard the front door to my right open and close, then Chyrel's voice. "If you value what's between your legs, Deputy, then kindly step aside."

Chyrel moved past me, then sat down next to Mason. "Are you okay?"

He nodded. "Yes, ma'am."

"Is it okay... if I..." the paramedic stammered.

"Yeah," Larry grunted, as he swung his injured left leg away so the boy couldn't see. "I don't think it's as bad as it looks."

Chyrel put an arm around the boy and pulled him close. He didn't resist. Having been molested by a drug dealer as a child and again later by a coach, combined with witnessing some gunplay, his teacher getting shot, and a man's body lying in the backyard, the poor kid seemed to have no will left to resist anything.

"Mr. McDermitt, may I speak with you?" a man behind me asked.

I looked back to see Sergeant Bruce. "Can it wait?"

"I'm afraid not." He turned and walked a few feet away.

Chyrel nodded, rocking the boy gently as the paramedic removed the hasty bandage on Larry's leg.

I rose and walked to where Bruce stood.

"My name's Sergeant Robert Bruce," he said. "I work with Diane sometimes."

I looked past him, through the window, and saw her sitting with a uniformed deputy, also wearing sergeant stripes.

"How is she?" I asked. "Why do you have to keep her segregated?"

"Procedure," he replied. "Any time a law enforcement officer is involved in a shooting. Can you tell me what you saw?"

"You'll have to be more specific, Sergeant Bruce. I *see* everything all day."

He scowled. "I know your background, Mr. McDermitt. How about working *with* me here? Let's say from the time your airplane started up the ramp."

So, I recounted everything I saw and heard, in great detail, from the moment we topped the ramp until Diane knelt over the body.

"You're certain she identified herself?" he asked. "*And* that the deceased fired first?"

"She said who she was and ordered him to drop his weapon," I replied. "You'll find a bullet hole in my plane's vertical stabilizer where he shot at us. That was his *only* hit out of four shots. Both rounds she fired were solid kill shots. He couldn't have fired after her. He was already dead."

"And why did you turn suddenly to the left?" he asked.

I arched an eyebrow, as if it were obvious. "So Diane could open her door and return fire."

CHAPTER THIRTY-SEVEN

Larry had brought Mason to the Rusty Anchor, knowing that Rusty and I would be returning there. He'd also asked Chyrel to meet him there after school, so they could both introduce the boy to me. She'd been waiting out by the highway, stopped by the police, and prevented from entering.

The two men and the woman who'd taken everyone hostage had been demanding to be told where the treasure was, and everyone at the Anchor, not knowing anything about any treasure, thought they were drunk, high, or delusional.

Dink and Hannah, along with Mitzi, John, Sid, and Maddy, had been the only ones in the restaurant when Larry walked in with Mason, surprising the three.

Dink swore that Larry had stepped in front of the boy when the blond girl wheeled around and fired.

I looked over at Larry, being tended by the medic, as Dink told me how it unfolded.

"Your man's a bona fide hero, Jesse," Dink said. "A teacher."

Too many times in recent years, there'd been reports of school shootings all across the country. The hurt, anguish, and loss of life was heartbreaking, and many times the teachers had been among the dead, shielding their charges and protecting them with their lives.

All for a crummy wage that was barely above poverty level.

I returned to where Chyrel sat, still holding Mason, and took the chair beside her. "I want you to give every teacher at the school a raise," I said, my voice low but firm. "Starting salary should be what a public school principal earns and go up from there by seniority."

Mason turned his head and looked up at me, holding my gaze. "Are you the principal?"

"Jesse founded the school," Chyrel explained. "Larry and Lauren were two of our first students."

His eyes turned sad, but he still held my gaze. "Did something bad happen to you too?"

I nodded slowly, feeling this kid's pain deep in the pit of my stomach. He'd been through the unimaginable, yet he was concerned for me and what I'd survived.

The back door opened, and I heard the familiar sound of large claws on the wood floor, followed by the quick steps of bare feet.

Tank approached, sniffing the air as he looked around at everyone, seeing Larry being tended to, and the sad eyes of Chyrel and Mason. He gently placed his big head on my knee, dark eyes looking up at the boy as his tail lightly smacked the table leg.

"Is that your dog?" Mason asked, a spark of light coming to his eyes.

Lauren rushed past us to go to Larry's side as I felt Savannah's warm hand on my shoulder.

"His name's Tank," I replied, as Alberto leaned against me. "And this is my son, Alberto, and my wife, Savvy—that's short for Savannah. Larry and Lauren live with us on our island."

He reached a tentative hand out to Tank's big, droopy jowl, and Tank leaned into his touch, allowing the boy to rub the soft fur behind his ear.

"He's kinda big," Mason said.

"He's *very* big," Alberto agreed. "He pulls me through the water on a kneeboard."

Mason looked over at Alberto. "Really?"

"Yeah, we have lots of fun," Alberto replied, his demeanor different than when he talked to adults. "Maybe you can try it with me one of these days. Mom, Dad, Larry, and Lauren are okay to be around, but I'm the only kid on our island."

Before Mason could respond, the paramedic stood up and announced, "It was just a flesh wound. I applied a coagulant and closed it with some butterfly bandages, but you'll still have to be transported to the hospital. We have to do that with any gunshot wound, but odds are, the doc there will change this bandage, check my work, rebandage it, and send you home."

"The burning's gone," Larry said. "Thanks, Doc."

"I'm just a paramedic, sir," the young man said, as he packed up his emergency kit. "I applied a topical anesthesia. By the time it wears off, the pain should be a lot more manageable." He glanced out the window, to where an ambulance had just parked. "Here comes the gurney now."

"Is that necessary?" Larry asked, then looked at Dink. "Can I just borrow your stick for a minute?"

The paramedic shook his head as two men came through the front door carrying a gurney. "Sorry. It's the rules."

I looked over at Larry, then rose and went to him, snatching Dink's intricately carved walking stick—a gift from Maddy.

I put the stick in Larry's hand and helped him to his feet. "Rules are made to be broken, son. Let the man have his dignity."

Lauren took her husband's other arm as Larry steadied himself with the walking stick, and we moved to the door, the EMT protesting loudly.

I glowered at the young man. "Step aside, son. Or join him in the back."

The others followed us outside as the paramedic was joined by two ambulance guys, and all three continued to fuss at Larry the whole way as we trudged slowly across the yard to the waiting ambulance.

He'd lost some blood, but not enough to make him woozy, and the pain was manageable. I believed that if a man were able, he should always do for himself. And I sensed Larry wanted the boy to know that.

"Dink told me what you did," I whispered to him.

"Did about what?" he asked, as the two ambulance guys got ahead of us to wait by the open rear doors.

"How you stepped in front of Mason," I replied, "when the girl started shooting."

"I did what?"

I grinned at him as the two men each reached to take an elbow and help him up. "You're on paid sick leave," I said. "I want you to spend some time with that kid and show him that not all men are creeps and cowards."

Larry pulled his arm from the grasp of one of the men and turned to face me. "Can you arrange a guys' night on the island?"

"Maybe another time," Lauren said, soothingly. "You're hurt."

Larry looked at Mason, standing off to the side with Chyrel, Savannah, Alberto, and Tank. "We don't know what hurt is, Lauren. I think Jesse's right. He needs positive male role models, and the courage to fight back."

"And you're just the one for the job," I said, nudging him toward the open doors. "Lauren will go with you and when you're done, I'll come and pick you up."

"I have an idea," Chyrel said. "How about you and Larry invite some friends over for a campout, and Savannah and Lauren can come and stay with me and the girls?"

The school still didn't have adequate housing for all the students, and Chyrel often took in the overflow.

"I think that's a wonderful idea," Savannah said. "We can take the girls shopping." She turned to me. "Call Deuce and see if he and Tony can come down. This is important for Larry."

"Make it happen for me?" Larry asked. "Mason needs to learn to not be afraid." Then he turned to Rusty. "Will you come?"

"Pshaw," Rusty said, grinning at Mason and Alberto. "I'll bring the root beer and hot dogs."

CHAPTER THIRTY-EIGHT

As the ambulance disappeared under the canopy of vegetation that covered the driveway, I turned and saw the boy, standing between Chyrel and Savannah, Tank sitting at his feet.

I pulled my phone out and glanced up at the sun. It'd been a long day already but there was still more than an hour of daylight left.

When Deuce answered, I said, "Can you and Tony be at my island in an hour?"

Deuce never asked questions unless they were mission-specific.

"What do you need us to bring?" he asked in a serious tone.

I moved away from the group and spoke quietly, explaining what had happened, who Mason was, and what had happened to him.

"We'll be there in less than an hour," Deuce said and ended the call just as Bruce approached me.

"Diane told me everything," he said. "About the gold you and your friends recovered."

That's all? I wondered.

I could tell Bruce was a no-nonsense kind of cop, one who always went by the book. I decided if she had also told him about the previous attack, he'd be reaching for his handcuffs.

"The gold's safe and not going anywhere," I replied. "It's under lock and key, inside a ten-foot, barbed wire fence, with an advanced and monitored security system in place."

"In a hangar at the airport," he said. "She told me."

"And you want to collect it tonight?" I surmised. "Evidence."

He glanced toward Diane, sitting on the deck with two uniformed deputies. "The two suspects are Will and Lena Crittenden," he replied, "and they said the dead man was their brother, Kevin. Diane said that you believe they are the great-grandchildren of a German submarine captain, and that you and your friends found the submarine and the gold it contained." He paused. "Your suspicions notwithstanding, *at this time*, there's no connection between the two suspects we apprehended and the case Diane was working in the Everglades with FWC. For now we're treating them as two separate investigations, and the gold is her case, not mine."

I arched an eyebrow questioningly. "What are you saying? Is she being arrested?"

"No," he replied immediately. "This is just procedure. Right now she's talking with the chaplain about what happened. She's still the primary case agent on the shooting of the FWC officers, at least until FDLE steps in. They'll eventually be taking over both cases. I'll have her contact you tomorrow about collecting the evidence."

I already knew that the Florida Department of Law Enforcement investigates all officer involved shootings, but I had a feeling that when this was all said and done, the FBI would become involved, because of the gold.

"Then we're free to go?"

"Just don't leave the state," he said, then grinned. "And don't move the gold."

"Nobody knows where it is," I said, "Except us, and now you and Diane. It'll be safe."

I thanked him, then returned to the others. "How about we get out of here and go someplace quiet?"

"Y'all go ahead," Chyrel said. "Mason wants to go to the hospital and wait for Mr. Larry."

I dropped to one knee in front of him. "Mr. Larry's going to be fine," I told him. "But he might need a little help getting around when he gets home. Think you can help him out?"

"I'll try," he replied, with very little conviction in his tone.

I put a hand on his shoulder. "When I was in the Marines, we didn't have a word for 'try.' The difficult things, we did right away, but the impossible took a little longer. Can you help Mr. Larry, son?"

His head came up and his eyes locked with mine. "Yes, sir."

I ruffled his hair. "Good then, because sometimes Larry's a malingerer."

"What's a ma... maleaner?"

"A *malingerer*," I replied with a wink, "is a Marine who spends too much time in sick bay."

The corners of his mouth turned up slightly, realizing I was pulling his leg. "He's not a malinger."

"So, you'll help him out?" I asked. "Bring him a root beer when he's thirsty, and help keep the bug fire going?"

"Bug fire?"

"We keep a small fire going all night," I replied. "Bugs get bad on our island after dark if we don't."

He nodded. "He saved my life."

I smiled openly and felt my left eye starting to sweat a little. "Want to know what I think?"

"What?"

"I think Mr. Larry sees something in you that's worth his time," I replied. "He sees someone who might one day change the world."

He looked down at the ground for a moment, and when he looked up again, his expression was a little different. I detected a glimmer of courage in his dark eyes. Maybe nobody had ever seen any worth in him before, except maybe as a punching bag or sexual object. He looked more... hopeful, I guess.

"I'll take care of him," he said in a small voice, but with all the seriousness he could muster.

"It's settled then," Chyrel said. "Mason and I will go pick up Mr. Larry and Ms. Lauren, then I'll bring them out to your place, and she and Savvy can ride back with me."

Rusty came trotting from the house, carrying a cooler, and with a go-bag slung over his shoulder. "Sid said I gotta be back by Friday mornin'," he said. "To get ready for the safari. Oh, and I called Billy. He's on his way."

"What about Hoyt?" I asked.

Rusty chuckled. "Maybe he ain't as Thurman as his DNA says. He said he was beat and just wanted to sit by the water until bedtime. Sid's got him all set up in one of the guest rooms."

"Mind if I leave my plane here for a while?" I asked him.

"We can all help ya move it onto the pad," Dink suggested.

"Let's do it," Rusty added, heading toward the backyard.

Alberto showed Mason what to do, and we all heaved and pushed *Island Hopper* onto the concrete pad where she'd lived for several years.

Once we got her in place and tied down, Mason looked up at me and asked, "Can I go for a ride sometime?"

Alberto draped an arm over his shoulder in a big-brotherly way and said, "He'll even let you *fly* it."

CHAPTER THIRTY-NINE

By the time we reached the island in my Grady, the sun was nearing the horizon, and off to the north, the leading edge of the cold front could be seen low on the horizon. It was still far to the north, and the latest forecast had it moving at only five miles per hour and possibly stalling out before reaching the Keys.

But living on the island, we tried to avoid potential problems by addressing them as if they were imminent.

"It'll probably be dark when Chyrel gets here," I said to Savannah, as Tank and Alberto ran ahead of us to lay up firewood for the night.

"You know as well as I do there's going to be a full moon rising any minute," she said with a scoff. "And that weather to the north is at least five hours away."

"Maybe you, Lauren, and Chyrel should stay here, just the same."

She stopped and turned to face me, then glanced ahead to where Alberto and Tank were chasing one another through the sandy interior of the island. "I think Larry has a better idea what that young man needs right now," she replied. "Just like another little boy who needed your help. If you're worried, we'll go straight to her house and lock ourselves in." She looked to the north. "You'll have it much rougher than we will."

I chuckled. "Maybe we all ought to go to Chyrel's."

"This is gonna be fun," Rusty said, coming up behind us with his go-bag slung over his shoulder. "I can't remember the last time I camped out."

"Yeah, fun," I replied. "Until the storm gets here."

"Storm my ass," he said, grounding his bag. "Ain't you learnt nothin' from me all these years?"

"What are you talking about?" I asked.

"Why'd you go all the way out to Key Colony Beach to turn around before landin' that bird of yours in the bight?"

I shrugged. "The wind changed and was out of the northwest."

"And now?" he asked.

He was right. The typical easterly wind had changed over the last day, blowing out of the northwest due to the approaching front, but I could feel it at my back now—it'd clocked almost back around to the east.

"It's almost reversed since then," I replied, knowing what was coming next.

"Now why do ya suppose that is?" he asked, rhetorically, and grinned. "That's a low-pressure system you're seein' to the north. They rotate counterclockwise. That west wind you landed in was caused by the approachin' low. But what you been feelin' for the last hour or so is easterly—comin' from a high that's been formin' over Cuba the last two days and is movin' this way now."

I chuckled with the realization. Nature abhors a vacuum, and the high-pressure system would try to fill in the low.

"I guess I still have a lot to learn," I said.

Rusty picked up his bag again and started toward the foot of the pier. "Naw, bro, you just been preoccupied. All we're gonna get is some wind and light rain around eleven o'clock."

Savannah smiled but tried to cover it with her hand. "Sorry. You just got *old*-schooled."

Then she started laughing as she ran after the others.

She wasn't far off. During my time living in the Keys, I'd learned a lot about weather, the ebb and flow of the tides, the stars in the sky, and the people of the Keys.

But Rusty's knowledge was generational. His family had lived on these boney islands for well over a century. He instinctively knew things a meteorologist with a master's degree would envy.

"Alberto," I called after him. "Lay up that firewood and make sure to pick a good color."

As I started to follow them, I heard the sound of outboard engines approaching from the northeast. I stepped back aboard the Grady, put Rusty's cooler on the dock, then got the binos out of the little side cabinet in the console and trained them in the direction of the sound.

It was Deuce's new boat, a thirty-two-foot Pursuit with an enclosed center console and twin Yamaha 350s. It was running flat out at probably thirty knots as it turned into Harbor Channel. It slowed a little coming around Mac and Mel's island, then headed straight toward the south pier.

I put the binos away and clicked the button on the key fob to open the big doors under the house. With *Gaspar's Revenge* at the city marina, there'd be plenty of room for Deuce's Pursuit.

After starting the engine, I quickly untied the lines as it idled. Once loose, I motored the Grady into its berth under the right side of the house.

By the time I got it tied off and had walked around to the west side of the dock area, Deuce was just turning into my channel.

He idled straight into the enclosed space under the left side of the house, killing the engines as he neared the dock where I stood.

I took the line Tony handed me and held the boat away until they got fenders out, then we tied it off and I clicked the key fob again to close the doors.

"Thanks for coming," I said, shaking both of their hands.

"Deuce brought me up to speed," Tony said. "Poor kid's probably afraid of everyone."

"It was Larry's idea," I explained. "He's bringing Mason out here to live for a while, in their guestroom, and I guess he wanted to kick it off with some sort of macho sleepover—just the guys."

"Sounds like good enough reason to me," Tony said, as the hydraulics whirred, closing the doors. "Hanging out with a bunch of snake-eaters is always good for my soul. Any idea where the guy who… hurt him is?"

"I do," I replied. "And his time's short. Right now, there's a kid coming out here who needs to know not all men are dangerous."

"But, uh…" Tony began. "We kinda are."

CHAPTER FORTY

It was late afternoon before Chyrel arrived with Larry, Lauren, and Mason. The sun was almost to the horizon and looking to the north, the front seemed to stretch across the whole sky from horizon to horizon.

But it wouldn't interfere with the sunset, nor our plans for the evening. If it rained, it rained. The human body is waterproof, as long as you didn't stand on your head during a cloudburst.

Alberto had a good fire going in the pit, using driftwood that produced green and orange flames around the base— festive colors. He didn't know about Mason's past, only that he was a kid who needed help.

To his credit, he never asked why.

The light easterly wind carried smoke across the island, driving away the mosquitoes, or luring them to a fiery death in the flames. Either way was okay by me.

We were all sitting on the south pier watching the evening light show as Chyrel turned her boat into the channel. Deuce and I helped tie off, and I introduced Mason to the two newcomers.

"Are you ready to go?" Chyrel asked Savannah. "It looks like it might rain soon."

Savannah had already packed a bag for what looked like a week.

As the two boys and Lauren helped Larry, who was awkwardly using a pair of crutches in the sand, I heard the unmistakable drone of a radial engine to the north.

"That'll be Billy," I said, heading toward the foot of the pier after them.

"Is that your airplane?" Mason asked, seeing Billy's Beaver turning upwind out over Content Passage.

"That's my friend, Billy," I replied. "I've known him since I was your age."

"Wow," he said, looking up at me. "That's a long time."

Savannah laughed.

We got Larry settled into a chair by the fire. Mason looked around at all of us, a question in his eyes. "Why are all these people coming here?"

Larry reached out and put a hand on the boy's shoulder. "These are all good men, Mason," he replied. "Solid, hard-working, and reliable."

"Like you?" Mason asked him.

Larry smiled, though I could see he was still in some pain. "I take that as a great compliment, Mason. 'A man is known by the company he keeps.'"

"Aesop!"

"Very good," Larry said. "You *have* been paying attention in my class. We asked some of our friends out here to show you some support. I promise, you don't have anything to fear while you're here on this island."

"We'd better get out there," I said, then turned to Savannah. "And you ladies better get going."

Lauren squeezed her husband's shoulder. "Are you sure you don't need me—"

"I absolutely do," Larry said, patting her hand gently. "And always will. But I'm fine. Tonight's about *manly* things."

Alberto hunched over and grunted like an ape, which brought a laugh from Mason.

Deuce and Tony found places to sit by the fire as I kissed Savannah and we all said our goodbyes. Then Chyrel led her and Lauren to the south pier.

Rusty and I headed to the north pier, and though it was nearly dark, I spotted Billy as his floats touched down on the water.

In minutes, he brought his plane to the T-head of the dock, beyond *Taranis*, and we helped him secure the plane.

"Thanks for coming," I said, as Billy climbed down.

Alberto and Mason came running out to where we stood by the plane, Tank lumbering behind them, as if he were watching over both of them like a big brother.

In another eleven days, he'd be two and was now fully grown, weighing nearly 130 pounds. So he really was a sort of big brother.

"Is that the boy?" Billy asked Rusty, who nodded.

The kids stopped short; Mason's eyes were all over the plane until he noticed Billy with us.

"Mason," Rusty said, "this here's my and Jesse's good friend, Billy Rainwater. Billy, this's Mason Slate."

Billy's eyebrows came up. "Really? That is a *very* strong name."

Mason looked up at him. "Are you an Indian?"

Billy nodded. "I am chieftain of the Calusa People."

I could hear Chyrel's boat from across the island as the women pulled away from the south dock.

"Just us guys now," I said, then looked down at Mason. "Billy and I are blood brothers. And like me and Rusty, he's also a Marine. Why don't we get back to the fire and crack open some root beers."

When we got back to the fire pit, Tony was telling Larry a joke, and all three men erupted in laughter.

"Starting the party without us?" I asked, moving around the fire to a wooden chaise I'd built. "Have a seat anywhere, Billy. You know everyone."

With everyone seated, and Rusty passing out bottles of root beer, I called Tank over beside me. "Is the island secure, boy?"

He looked around, then chuffed a light bark.

"That means yes," Alberto said to Mason.

"He knows what your dad's saying?"

"He sure does," Alberto replied. "He's a really smart dog."

"And really big," Mason added.

Alberto draped an arm around Tank's broad shoulders. "Tomorrow, I can show you how to ride my kneeboard while he pulls you."

Mason turned to Larry. "Do you need anything, Mr. Larry?"

He smiled through the pain. "I think we have all the bases covered here, Mason. Good friends, good drink, a good fire, and good weather."

Just as he said it, the first drops of rain began to fall.

I looked over at Rusty. "I thought you said it wouldn't rain until nearly midnight."

He shrugged as he whittled the prongs on a forked stick. "Just a precursor," he said, then looked around at the others. "If y'all're gonna eat, you'd best get to cuttin' some cookin' sticks." He reached into a cooler and took out a package of hot dogs. "You want this'un, Mason?"

Rusty handed him the stick, skewered a dog with the prongs, and showed Mason where to hold it near the base of the fire, out of the flames.

"Slow is smooth," he told the boy. "And smooth is fast."

"What's that mean?"

"Well, if ya stuck that dog in the flame for a faster cook," Rusty began, "then it'll be all burnt on the outside and not cooked inside, so you'll have to start over. Ain't nothin' in life more time-consumin' than havin' to do somethin' twice."

Within seconds, the rest of us produced pocket knives and were whittling away on dried driftwood twigs.

Mason looked over at Tony, slowly turning his stick so the dog didn't burn. Then he looked at Deuce and asked, "Are you a Marine, too?"

Rusty laughed. "They're unintelligent squids, kiddo. Navy guys. Deuce and Tony both. But that's okay—they take us Marines to where the fightin' is."

"Keep it up, jarhead," Tony said without looking up.

I laughed, noting Mason's shocked expression. "Deuce and Tony were SEALs," I said. "The Navy's most elite warriors. We kid each other a lot, but Deuce is actually married to Rusty's daughter."

"And me and Jesse known each other so long, we're like brothers," Rusty added. "My Jules calls him uncle, but he's actually her godfather."

Tony looked across the fire at the boy, Tank now slumbering beside him. "I served under Deuce for a long time and have known Julie since she was a teenager. I think of her like she was my own little sister."

Rusty chuckled again. "First time me and Jesse met *this* guy," he said, nodding toward Deuce, "he was barely out of diapers. His pop was a close friend of me and Jesse."

"But when it comes to long-time friendship," Billy said. "Jesse and I have known each other more than half a century. Ever since we were six and seven years old." He smiled at the boy. "Jesse's the old man, though."

"It's good to have old friends around," Alberto said. "And new friends too."

CHAPTER FORTY-ONE

The rain finally did come in earnest an hour later as the two fronts collided. Yet it was a surprisingly warm rain, and the air temperature had remained near eighty, meaning the high-pressure system was winning out, bringing warm, moist air up out of the Caribbean.

We didn't seek shelter. We got wet, and the heat of the fire soon caused steam to rise from our clothes. We'd banked enough big chunks of driftwood and had a hot enough base of embers that it took a while for the rain to even begin to put it out.

We feasted on hot dogs, baked beans cooked in their cans, and fists full of chips, straight from the bags. We quaffed many root beers, and told stories, jokes, and life lessons learned until well past midnight. By then, the rain had stopped, and the fire came back, warming our wet clothes.

The island had always been a refuge, a place where the world's noise couldn't reach. Tonight, though, it carried a different weight. Every creak of the dock boards, every rustle of mangrove leaves, seemed to remind me that evil didn't always stay on the mainland. It had found its way to my shoreline before and could again. But on that particular night, evil would be wise to get right with Jesus before setting foot on the island. We were a bunch of heathens baying at the sky, and a few of us were genuine snake-eaters.

I knew we were safe on the island, if by virtue of numbers and nothing else. But it went far beyond that. The company we kept were the best of the best and as Tony had alluded to earlier, some of the most dangerous people on planet Earth.

Rain rolled down our faces, plastering our hair. We laughed, yelled up at the night sky, and basically behaved like a bunch of kids on a camping trip.

Larry had brought Mason to the island hoping the quiet tranquility and the camaraderie of old friends would help him breathe easier, relax, and understand that there were good people in the world.

In the firelight of the previous evening, I'd seen the boy had more color in his cheeks, but shadows still lingered behind his eyes the next morning.

Chyrel, Savannah, and Lauren returned before noon, and Chyrel went straight to the comm shack in the western bunkhouse to set up her computers, explaining only that she'd stumbled upon something the night before.

I brought her a fresh coffee as she sat at the desk in the comm shack, three laptops glowing around her like a war council. I'd never seen Chyrel work so intensely, and according to Savannah, she'd barely slept or eaten the night before.

On her screens, windows opened and closed quickly as she painstakingly pieced together a digital mosaic of crimes and communications.

I placed the coffee by her elbow.

She didn't look up. "His name's Dennis Carver, Jesse. You're gonna want to sit down for the rest."

I sat on the bunk next to the desk. "Hit me."

She tapped a key, and one of the screens filled with what looked like chat logs—online conversations under various "handles" Carver used.

To my thinking, the anonymity of the internet wasn't good. It allowed people to say and do things that they'd never do in real life.

I began to read, understanding a little about how pedophiles groomed and stalked young boys and girls online.

The texts were ugly things, threaded with unmistakable patterns, guarded language, intentional timing, and the twisted tactics of a predator.

"Notice the IP stamps," Chyrel said, pointing with a pencil. "They trace back to his home network and his office at the school. I've got service provider logs confirming usage down to the minute. No way he can claim somebody else was behind the keyboard."

I felt the knot in my stomach tighten. "Is it enough for the Bureau?"

"More than enough for the right agent," she replied. "And by that, I mean all this was gathered without a warrant… and it gets worse."

She switched to another screen, a folder of images. "There aren't any pictures of the kids here. He's too smart for that. These are his trophies—snapshots of identifiable locations, receipts, and travel itineraries. He's a compulsive record hoarder. He documents everything, and some of these times and locations line up with reports of juveniles who have gone missing."

My fists clenched. "How many?"

"Four confirmed," she said quietly. "Two more likely. All minors."

The screens blurred together for a second, forcing me to take a deep breath and blink hard. "Christ."

"That's not all," Chyrel went on. "He used a burn phone to coordinate meetings with his victims. Thought he was slick. I cloned the number from the cloud backups and pulled up its GPS logs. The data puts him within a mile of our school three different times since Mason came to us."

I closed my eyes tightly, jaw clenched. The guy was *stalking* Mason, even now.

Pedophiles are never fully rehabilitated.

The thought kept going around and around in my head. Mason was the latest in a long line of children this guy had abused, and he wasn't going to stop there.

If I hadn't already promised Savannah we'd let the system handle this, I'd have been tempted to settle it the old-fashioned way—with a match-grade, 175-grain, .308 round and a shallow, wet grave among the mangroves.

Instead, I opened my eyes and said, "Package everything. We're getting Diane out here."

"Mr. Stockwell's been briefed," she said, not looking up. "But this isn't an Armstrong investigation."

"I know," I replied, rising from the bunk. "And thanks."

When I called her, Detective Pine said she could come within a couple of hours and true to her word, she arrived before noon in a borrowed skiff that was only a small step up from the folding boat she'd come out here in once before.

Her face was set in the kind of no-nonsense expression that had probably rattled more than a few criminals in Monroe County.

She carried a leather satchel and a body camera, and the first thing she said when she stepped onto the dock was, "You better tell me you've got something solid, Jesse."

Chyrel stepped toward her and handed Diane a thumb drive and a stack of printouts. "Solid? Honey, this is bedrock. I'm Chyrel. Glad to finally meet you in person."

Diane's eyes showed surprise as she turned toward me. "So this is an Armstrong—"

"Freelance," Chyrel interrupted. "Zero oversight."

The three of us crossed the island's interior to the north pier, where *Taranis* was docked. I could hear Alberto and Mason playing in the shallows with Tank. They stopped and watched us go between the bunkhouses.

We settled at *Taranis's* inside dinette for more room, and Chyrel spread the evidence across the table and plugged in her laptop.

Larry and Mason boarded and hovered in the cockpit, the boy fidgeting with Tank's collar as Chyrel laid everything out in chronological order for Diane.

Finally, she looked up, then out at Mason. "I'll have to talk to him," she said, softening her voice. "I'll need a formal statement."

I went through the slider and crouched down beside Mason. "You're not gonna have to do anything you don't want, kid," I said gently. "Do you remember last night? We're all brothers now. Nobody's gonna make you stand up in a courtroom or face him again. But Detective Pine needs to hear from you, in your own words, about what happened. Just once, then it's done."

Mason bit his lip, eyes fixed on the deck. Tank nudged his hand with a wet nose, and the boy managed a faint smile.

Larry knelt on his other side. "You're safe here, Mason. We'll be right beside you."

He swallowed hard, then gave a small nod. "Okay. I can do it."

CHAPTER FORTY-TWO

We set things up in the salon, just Mason, Diane, and the body camera. Larry and I stood right behind him, close enough that he felt our presence.

Larry had started the previous night's more painful discussions, and one by one, each of us talked about events in our lives that'd been traumatic, things that had shaped us as men. Alberto spoke of his mother's murder and his being set adrift in a leaky skiff, and at the end, we'd all sworn a brotherhood and called ourselves the Fire Watchers, though most of us had considered our relationships to be one of brotherhood anyway.

Larry and I listened to Mason's monotone responses and descriptions in silence.

It wasn't easy. His words broke now and then, and he needed long pauses. Larry and I stood close by him the whole time, filling the salon with quiet self-assurance.

Mason found his courage. He told Diane what Carver had said, what he'd *tried* to do, what he *did* do, and how it made him feel. Not in graphic detail—Diane was careful with her questions—but enough to draw a clear and damning picture of the man.

When he finished, the boy let out a breath like he'd been holding it for months. Diane stopped the recording and put her hand on his shoulder. "You did good, Mason. You did *real* good. We'll take it from here."

Lauren and Savannah had tears in their eyes when Mason came out into the cockpit. He leaned against Lauren, exhausted, but lighter somehow, like he'd set down a pack he'd been carrying for way too long.

"Can I take a nap?" he asked Savannah sheepishly.

"Of course," she replied, then led him down into *Taranis's* port ama and the guest cabin there.

I stepped down onto the dock, where Deuce, Tony, Billy, and Rusty waited.

"He looks spent," Deuce said.

I stepped past him. "I need a drink."

The four of them followed me out to the fire pit, where Rusty pulled a bottle of Pussers from his cooler and handed it to me.

I pulled the cork and took a deep pull on the bottle, feeling the amber liquid burn its way down my throat. No glass, no ice, no mixer.

The five of us sat down, and I passed the bottle to Billy as I began recounting what I'd heard Mason relay to Diane.

None of us drank much these days, and it was barely afternoon, but the situation called for a little numbing of the mind, so we passed the bottle around.

"She thinks it'll stick?" Tony asked.

"She says it's the strongest case she's seen in years," I replied. "And with Mason's statement she can get a warrant to gather the same evidence on her own, legally. Carver's done. He won't see daylight for a long time, if ever."

"And every day for him will be a living hell," Billy added. "Inmates take a dim view of child molesters."

Rusty corked the rum bottle. "Good. Damn good. Kid deserves that."

"Mason will get justice the *right* way," I added.

Rusty nodded. "Chyrel sure can be one mean geek when she needs to be, bro."

"No doubt," Tony confirmed. "She's scary good."

For the first time in a long time, I smiled as I looked into the flames, feeling like maybe—just maybe—the system might actually work.

THE SUN WAS ALMOST TO ITS ZENITH WHEN DIANE LEFT THE island with the evidence package tucked inside her leather satchel. Savannah came across the lawn as the sound of Diane's outboard faded into the distance.

"She's taking it to the Bureau." she said, taking a seat beside me. "She spoke to the DA and they both agree Mason's statement gives them probable cause."

I nodded. "Straight to the Miami field office. If they've got half the brain cells they should, they'll put their best people on it."

Rusty leaned forward, elbows on his knees. "Best people, huh? You mean the ones who show up late, write a stack of reports, and claim credit after the dust settles?"

"Sometimes," I admitted. "But not always." My phone chirped and I pulled it out. "Speak of the devil."

I pressed the *Accept* button. "Hey, Diane. Did you forget something?"

"Sheena Chambers," she said through the hiss of water and outboard noise. "Do you know her?"

The name hit me like a jab to the ribs, except her last name had been Mason when we'd met—a strange coincidence now. Sheena wasn't a common name, though. I doubted there'd be more than two or three in the whole Bureau, let alone the Miami field office.

We'd gone our separate ways years earlier, but the mention of her name still carried weight.

"Yeah," I said slowly. "I know her. Good field agent. And best of all, she knows how we work."

"Armstrong?"

"Something like that," I replied.

"I just got off the phone with her," Diane said. "She's flying down tomorrow and will want to meet you. All of you. This is going federal now, and things are going to move fast."

"We can meet at the Rusty Anchor," I said. "What time's she arriving?"

"She said she'll be wheels up at sunrise."

"We'll all be there at 0800," I replied, then we ended the call.

"Someone you know?" Savannah asked.

"From a lifetime ago," I replied and managed a smile. "Pre-you."

It was a song by the late Jimmy Buffett, where the troubadour tries to explain to his girlfriend about another woman they'd bumped into.

It'd already been a long day, at the end of a long week, in what should have been a quiet period following Thanksgiving.

Only it wasn't quiet.

Diane didn't say to bring the boy, but knowing Sheena's methodologies, I assumed she'd at least want to ask him, in person, to verify the statement he'd given Diane.

We busied ourselves throughout the afternoon, mundane chores that could be done with the mind on autopilot, shared cooking tasks, pulling lobster traps, picking vegetables from the garden, whatever it took to pass the time.

When Mason was up and about again, the boys played with Tank, taking turns being pulled on the kneeboard.

The sun continued its slow, inexorable march across the sky.

Deuce and Tony left before sunset, borrowing Billy's Wi-Fi enabled long-range camera. Deuce wanted to find Carver and sit on him, surveilling him from a distance, to make sure he didn't somehow get wind of something and try to run.

The rest of us decided to turn in shortly after sunset so we could get an early start for the Rusty Anchor the next morning.

We said our goodnights and headed up to our house.

Alberto paused at the door to his room.

"Dad?"

His back was to me. "Yes, Son?"

"Did somebody hurt Mason?"

"Yes, they did," I replied quietly. "Very badly, but in a way that doesn't show on the outside."

"Are you going to fix it?"

Savannah looked up at me, her eyes welling.

Fixing things is what I did. Whether it was a busted lobster trap, a fishing reel, a malfunctioning autopilot, or evil's encroachment on civilized society, it was inherent in my DNA to correct the problems.

"*We* are going to fix it, Son," I replied. "All of us."

CHAPTER FORTY-THREE

We gathered at the Rusty Anchor the next morning. Chyrel had just a single laptop set up at a corner table, the louvered windows behind her fully closed. Nobody bothered her.

Rusty sat at the bar chewing on a toothpick, and Savannah and Maddy brewed coffee like it was ammunition for a siege.

I paced. I hated waiting.

I was just turning away from the door when it opened and Sheena Chambers walked in. It felt like time had folded in on itself. She looked the same, tall, poised, sharp-eyed, but with a few more lines around her mouth, the kind that came from years of chasing predators and talking to liars.

"Jesse," she said with a simple nod.

I swallowed. "Sheena."

No hug, no handshake, just a brief nod that might or might not carry a thousand unspoken words.

Savannah caught it all, of course. She raised an eyebrow but said nothing. They'd met before, years ago, but I couldn't tell if either remembered the other.

I introduced Sheena to Diane and explained that what she was about to review was gathered without a warrant.

"That won't be a problem," Diane said. "I submitted the victim statement to the DA and he's got us a warrant for a digital search already." She nodded toward where Chyrel sat. "It was just a matter of knowing where to look."

Sheena glanced from Diane to me. "Still stepping over the rules?"

"I'll go over, around, dig my way under, or just blast right through when the welfare of a kid is at stake," I replied. "Mason's outside playing with my dog."

"I'll be able to pull all of this same evidence myself before noon," Diane continued. "Or at least our tech people will. But I want to bring federal charges, and after you hear his statement and see the evidence, I'm sure you'll agree."

Sheena smiled at her. "It's rare that local law enforcement is so eager to turn a case over."

"I'm no fool, Agent Chambers," Diane said. "I want this guy to go down hard, but out of professional courtesy, I'd ask to remain part of the investigation all the way to the end."

"Show me what you've got," Sheena said, and they both sat down with Chyrel.

Diane and Chyrel spread the files across the table, one side illegally obtained and the other side through proper channels. Every now and then, the printer in Rusty's office would whir and Savannah would bring out another stack of papers for the "legal" side of the table.

"This is what Chyrel pulled," Diane began. "It's a mountain of digital evidence, all of which will be sent to me by my tech people as they receive it. Mason Slate gave a statement that lines up with communications between him and the perp. It paints a pretty ugly picture. We're looking at multiple charges; abuse, exploitation, travel with intent, possession of materials... not to mention almost certain involvement in a number of cases involving missing children. Enough to get him life without parole, even as we investigate the possible homicides."

"Florida still has the death penalty," Sheena reminded her. "Why not wait and build the murder cases?"

"We have him solid for this," Diane replied. "We can always add charges later. We don't want this guy to figure out we're onto him, then disappear."

"The death penalty is too damned easy," Chyrel said with great conviction.

Sheena scanned the printouts, her eyes narrowing. "Dennis Carver," she murmured. "I've seen his name before."

"Background check?" I asked. "He's a public school teacher up in your neck of the woods."

She shook her head slowly as she continued to look over the documents. "Internal referral. Two years ago, we got a tip about a coach trading files online. Never enough to pin anything on him, though. We shelved the investigation when the trail went cold. But this..." She tapped the stack of evidence. "This ties a bow on it."

Chyrel leaned back, smug. "You're welcome."

Sheena almost smiled. "Whoever you are, remind me never to end up on your bad side."

Rusty chuckled. "Join the club."

After Sheena reviewed the video statement, she asked to speak to Mason for just a minute.

She smiled at the boy and thanked him after verifying that the recording was him. "You're a brave young man," she said. "What you've done will probably prevent something bad from happening to someone else. I have a little boy a few years younger than you. So you have my personal thanks, as well."

When she was finished, I walked Sheena out to a Monroe

County patrol car that had been idling in the parking lot the whole time. The deputy at the wheel sat up straighter as we approached.

"You look good, Jesse," Sheena murmured.

"So do you."

A long pause.

"It looks like you have a lot of friends here," she said. "A life. I'm glad."

I didn't know what to say to that, so I just nodded.

"Carver won't know what hit him," she went on. "But we need to be careful and still move fast. If he suspects the investigation, he could rabbit. Or worse, he could hurt another kid before we close in."

"I'm a partner in a private investigation firm up island," I said. "I have two of my guys up there. They already have eyes on him. Quiet; just enough to make sure he doesn't spook."

"Who are they?" she asked. "Or do I *not* want to know?"

"My partner, Deuce Livingston," I replied. "Retired SEAL team leader and former Assistant Deputy Director of Homeland Security. With him is one of his SEAL teammates, Tony Jacobs. You've met them both."

"No more than them," she said. "I know you, Jesse. And I know how you and your friends work. I'm surprised the man's still alive after seeing and hearing what I have."

I gave her a crooked grin. "There are worse things."

She studied my face for a moment. "Still can't stay out of the fight, can you?"

"Not when it involves kids," I replied.

"That other boy," she said. "Who's he?"

"My and Savannah's adopted son," I replied. "His mom was murdered by gangbangers up on the mainland."

She mustered a sad smile as she opened the passenger door of the patrol car, then glanced toward the bar. "I recognized her. Tell her I said hello."

I nodded.

"I'll have two of my agents take over surveillance with my next phone call," she said, but it wasn't like it was an offer. "I'll let you know when to pull your guys off."

Deuce and Tony had already reported in a couple of times, with long-lens still photos and short videos from Billy's camera.

I said goodbye to Sheena, and before the dust from the patrol car settled, I got another text from Deuce with an attached video.

As Rusty and Hoyt approached, I played the video and watched Dennis Carver striding around what looked like a school gym, whistle around his neck, and belly hanging over his belt. Boys in headgear circled the mats. He laughed with some of them, instructed others, slapped shoulders, and played the part of the friendly coach.

But I knew the truth.

Rusty watched the video over my shoulder, muttering, "Son of a bitch looks like somebody's favorite uncle or some such shit."

"That's how they do it," Hoyt added coldly, standing beside his cousin. "Blend in. Pretend to care. All the while looking for the next kid to corner. I was a youth pastor for a while, working with kids in foster care."

"Deuce'll be on him like glue," I replied.

"Don't I know it," Rusty agreed. "My grandsons go to school not far from there. The man's fixated when it comes to his two boys."

We went back inside, and while we waited for updates from Deuce, Sheena, or Diane's people, Rufus brought out some food. The updates started coming quickly.

Diane got a call, telling her the warrant had come through for a digital search as well as a tap on Carver's burn phone, regular cell phone, and his office extension at the school. Then she, too, left, headed for Miami with her warrants.

When I went back in again, Rusty was behind the bar, polishing a perfectly spotless beer mug, much the same as his dad had done.

"Remind you of another time?" he asked.

I nodded somberly. "Hurry up and wait."

CHAPTER FORTY-FOUR

I paced the floor some more. Waiting wasn't my strong suit—not by a nautical mile—but I'd done more than my fair share of waiting when I was in the Corps. Sometimes, we had to get ready quickly for something, only to wait long hours to even start waiting to get word about it.

Hence the term "hurry up and wait."

I needed to be active, doing *something*, but there was nothing to do but wait. So I paced.

Pacing was doing something.

A few patrons came in, casting furtive glances at those of us in the corner. They somehow felt the tension in the air and didn't approach any of us. And Maddy made sure to seat anyone as far from Chyrel's table as possible.

Sheena, Diane, Deuce, and Tony were all linked directly to Chyrel's laptop's communications network, which was run through her new and improved METIS connection to the Armstrong mainframe.

Deuce reported Carver's activities to me every fifteen minutes, copying Chyrel with his texts, videos, and photos as Carver went about his day, then locked up the gym to go to his fourth period algebra class.

Routine, Deuce reported. *He's a creature of habit.*

Which makes him predictable, I typed back.

And makes him catchable, Tony added to the group text.

Sheena called while the boys were out back with Tank, and I put her on speaker so the others could hear, but turned the volume down so those at the other end of the dining area and at the bar couldn't.

"We're filing for a warrant based on the digital evidence Detective Pine has already gathered," Sheena said. "She's on her way here now with two Monroe County units as backups. We'll get the warrants, I'm sure, and once we have them, we'll hit his condo, his office, his car... everything. Every device he owns comes with us. We already know what we'll find, but we need it clean. Ironclad."

"And until then?" Savannah asked.

"We keep him under surveillance," Sheena replied, as another text from Deuce came in. "Discreetly. We can't risk him sniffing something in the wind. One wrong move, and he disappears. You can pull your guys off now, Jesse. My agents are in position."

I opened the text and grinned. "Can your guys see mine?"

"They haven't reported anyone snooping around, if that's what you mean."

"My guys have already spotted yours," I said. "Tell them to lose the coats and ties. And tell the blond guy his shoe's untied. My guys will stay on location. Quiet. No cowboy stunts."

Rusty smirked. "Speak for yourself."

"Some things never change," Sheena said, then ended the call.

I trusted Deuce and Tony. They knew how to blend in, move around, and not be noticed. Skills the two Bureau guys in the still photo needed to brush up on.

Though it was early December, the high-pressure dome out of Cuba brought some afternoon heat, pressing down on the Middle Keys like a hand, heavy and damp.

Hanging from the rafters in the Rusty Anchor, three large ceiling fans spun lazily, pushing air around that smelled faintly of the ocean and coffee. Each revolution of the one in the center produced a slight squeak.

Nobody spoke much, not while we waited.

The whole gang clustered around the table where Chyrel had her computer set up. The cooling fan on the laptop hummed, the screen danced with maps, chat windows, and phone logs flashing past. She wore an earwig, half-listening for pings from her digital world signaling new information coming in.

Rusty wiped away invisible smudges on the bar top, stopping occasionally to stare at the muted TV screen over the bar.

Savannah brewed another pot of coffee, even though none of us needed more. We were all on edge.

The only one not fidgeting with impatience was Billy, sitting quietly at Chyrel's table, back to the wall, his face the ever-present stoic mask of generations of his people.

When I passed near the table, he looked up. "Sit, Kemosabe."

I spun a chair around and straddled it, grinning at him. "I've known you damned near my whole life," I said. "And I've never seen you this excited."

He grinned back at the jab. "The mind can be active without the body's participation."

"Ancient Calusa wisdom?"

He shrugged. "Trish."

My phone buzzed on the table. Group text. Deuce.

Carver just finished his 5th-period class. Tony's across the lot. He's on schedule, nothing weird.

I tapped back a quick note with one finger.

Eyes sharp. Head on a swivel.

Rusty was reading my text upside down. "Deuce don't miss anything. Boy's like a bloodhound with bifocals."

I ignored him and looked to Chyrel. "Anything new?"

"Still got him triangulated," she replied. " burn phone's on but idle, and he's logged into the school Wi-Fi under his admin account, probably checking internal emails. You want me to scrape them live?"

"No," I said. "Wait for the warrant. Diane needs everything clean at this point."

As if summoned, my phone chirped in my hand. It was Diane. I answered on speaker.

"A federal judge is reviewing the paperwork now," Diane said, her voice tight. "With Mason's statement and the digital trail, there's no reason it won't go through. I've already prepped deputies for standby to assist as needed. They're parked half a mile from the school, and I'm riding with Sheena for the duration."

Sheena's voice came through faintly in the background, sharp and steady. "Tell Jesse we'll have paper before the final bell. I want him in cuffs at that school, not a chance to vanish."

Savannah looked down at me, her features fierce as she placed two mugs on the table for me and Chyrel, and handed Billy a bottle of water.

"Trish texted me," she said to Billy. "Don't forget to do your eyedrops."

He glanced at the big clock over Rusty's office door, then pulled a small vial from his pocket. "Thanks."

Billy suffered from glaucoma, an irreversible disease of the optic nerve, and the eyedrops helped to keep it from progressing.

I looked at the clock. It was 1400. Two hours till dismissal. Two hours to get the warrants signed and teams in place.

I resumed pacing.

At 1430, another buzz from my phone. Video from Tony. I thumbed it open.

It showed Carver, striding through the gym, whistle around his neck, slapping boys on the butt when they did well. Lots of coaches did it, but the sight of this turd fondler doing it turned my stomach.

Rusty muttered, "He's got no clue the noose is already around his neck."

"Hopefully he stays that way," I said.

At 1515, Diane called again. This time her voice carried a different tone. "Signed," she reported. "All of it. Digital seizures, hardware, software, physical arrest, the works. The judge even stated that he wants Carver off the streets before the sun goes down. Sheena's team is rolling now. And since the complainant is now a resident custodial minor going to school in Monroe County, she's asked if I'd like to join her for the arrest. One of my deputies is coordinating right now with the school's on-site resource officer."

Chyrel whooped, throwing her pencil into the air. "Yes! That's the nail in his coffin."

A few patrons looked our way, but weird outbursts and antics weren't unusual among Keys locals.

I leaned forward, elbows on the table. "Deuce and Tony are already there, on the east side of the lot in a black Suburban close to Carver's SUV. Put Sheena's agents on the west side. We want him boxed in before he even thinks about leaving."

Rusty grinned. "You mean we're finally moving?"

"We're moving," I replied, watching Mason and Alberto throwing a football out back.

Updates came fast after that.

Deuce texted, *School day ending. He's packing up the gym, talking to two other coaches. Still smiling. No sign he suspects a thing.*

Another from Tony. *Feds rolling in. Parking like they belong. Carver hasn't noticed.*

Chyrel scanned her screen. " burn phone just lit up. Text message sent to three unknown numbers. Nothing shady, just says 'practice is canceled, see you Monday.' Looks like he's trying to clear his schedule. Probably thinks he's got a weekend to himself."

Rusty chuckled. "Yeah, he's got a hot date with a 300-pound ape in the hoosegow."

At 1545, Sheena's voice came through on the open line I had with Diane, sounding calm and certain. "Warrants are in hand and my teams are in position. We'll let him walk toward his vehicle, then intercept before he touches the door handle. No chance for resistance, no chance for destruction of evidence, and no chance of escape."

Rusty slapped the bar with an open palm. "Hell *yes*! Bring him down."

I felt the room shift. Tension broke, replaced by sharp focus. It was happening.

"Ask Jesse if he has other guys here now," Sheena said. "Over there beyond Deuce's Suburban."

I shook my head, though she and Diane couldn't see me. "They're not mine. They look like cops, though."

CHAPTER FORTY-FIVE

The three men moved as one. They were dressed South Florida casual, with light coats, typical for a teacher this time of year. Only they were trying a little too hard to look the part.

It didn't matter. Dennis Carver didn't have a single damned clue, but I went around to look at Chyrel's screen anyway.

She had a live-stream from Sheena's dash-cam on the monitor, and I could see Deuce's black, up-armored SUV on the right, halfway down a row of cars. Three men were walking casually into the parking lot just beyond it. They were trying hard to appear casual but moved like cops.

I grinned, wishing I could be there personally.

Probably just as well that I wasn't, though. Even with all those cops around, I doubt I could restrain myself from choking the life out of Carver.

The image on Chyrel's laptop was sharp and crystal clear, but it was a wide angle, high-definition lens, which made everything look farther away, and the hood of the car impossibly long.

Still, I could pick out two, possibly three, other cars, two of which I could see had two occupants, which I pegged for government-issued vehicles.

Chyrel confirmed it, pointing with her pencil at each of the cars in turn. "FBI guys are here, here, and here." Then she pointed at a green mini-van. "That's Carver's SUV, and there he comes."

Carver was easily recognizable in his red coach's shorts and matching hat, and he still had the stupid whistle around his neck, strolling toward his car without a care. He carried a small leather briefcase that didn't suit the wardrobe at all.

"Everybody hold," Sheena said. "Suspect is in sight. Red shorts and hat, yellow shirt. Wait for him to get closer. Who are those guys? Anyone?"

The three men who'd been walking toward Carver to intercept suddenly turned and drew weapons, pointing them at Deuce's Suburban.

"Wrong truck!" I snarled, reaching for my phone, knowing it was already too late.

"Guns!" I heard Diane and Sheena shout as one. "Go, go, go!"

Then all hell broke loose.

The three men started firing at the passenger side of Deuce's Suburban where Tony sat, unleashing a murderous barrage.

At the same time, the doors of all three Bureau cars flew open as Sheena and Diane sprinted forward, away from the dash-cam.

In seconds, it was all over. Two agents threw Carver to the ground, shielding him with their own bodies as they put the cuffs on him.

He offered no resistance.

Four other agents, along with Diane and Sheena, surrounded the three men, just as two patrol cars skidded to a stop on either side.

I couldn't make out any features of the three men, as they were quickly disarmed, and taken down to the ground where they were forced onto their stomachs.

I grinned when Tony's door opened and he came out with his

SIG Sauer P226 pointed down at the three men, and holding up his credentials with his other hand, all while he shouting at the men on the ground.

"Who the hell are those guys?" I demanded from anyone who could tell me.

Nobody answered.

Carver was hoisted to his feet and marched by two deputies back toward Sheena's car as two agents lifted one of the three shooters to his feet to be escorted to another car.

"I know him," Maddy said. "That guy they just took away to the left. He was right here drinking a beer just last night."

The three men had tried to look casual, but being professionals, that was hard, and it was their wariness that had given them away to me.

I picked up my phone and called Diane. On the screen, I could see her pull her phone out and hold it to her ear as they followed Carver.

"We got him, Jesse," she announced. "Three men tried to interfere but we—"

"Be sure to tow Deuce's truck," I said, interrupting her. "Pull the slugs from the bulletproof glass and have ballistics look at them alongside those you got from the bodies of Kim's FWC guys."

She stopped walking, turned, and looked back. "Wait, you mean... How could you possibly know?"

"Just a hunch," I replied. "Deuce has been using Billy's camera to upload pictures and videos directly through a Wi-Fi connection. The guys who hit the sub were pros and they had technical backup. They might have tracked the camera, thinking it was Billy."

I heard the sound of the car door open through the laptop's

speaker and a man saying, "I don't have anything to do with those guys. I've never seen them before in my life."

There was a thump and a groan as the car rocked slightly. I grinned, knowing that someone had "accidentally" bumped Carver's head in the door frame while putting him in the backseat.

Then Sheena's no-nonsense voice could be heard. "Dennis Carver, I'm Special Agent Sheena Chambers with the FBI. I'm placing you under arrest for felony child abuse. You have the right to remain silent. Anything you say can and will be used against you in a court of law. You have the right to an attorney. If you cannot afford an attorney, one will be provided for you. Do you understand these rights?"

"Well... yeah. But like I said, I don't know those guys. I'm a *teacher* here."

His last words fell on deaf ears as the car door was slammed shut,

Diane and Sheena met at the front of the car, looking over to the other shooters now being cuffed into the patrol cars.

"Stupid-ass cops," Carver muttered over the dash-cam's open microphone. "I have somewhere to be and not a lot of time left. You're screwing up months of work on this kid."

Chyrel looked up at me. "The dash-cam is two-way audio-enabled, Jesse. Would you like to say something?"

I nodded and bent close to the small desk microphone by Chyrel's right elbow, gripping the little stalk tightly as she tapped a few keys, then nodded.

"Can you hear me, Carver?" I asked, keeping my voice low.

"Who's that?" he asked.

"Never mind who I am," I replied. "Just know this. A little boy named Mason Slate sends his regards, and I'm going to *personally* do everything in my power to see that your cellmate is the biggest, ugliest, most sadistic inmate they have at Sumterville."

I sliced my hand across my throat, and Chyrel ended the two-way connection.

EPILOGUE

Two Weeks Later, December 20

It was Saturday afternoon, just five days before Christmas, and a little over two weeks since Dennis Carver had been arrested. All six of us from the island had piled into Larry's boat for the ride to the Rusty Anchor for the weekly lionfish safari.

Mason had stayed with us on the island, accepting Larry and Lauren's offer of their small guest room. We'd stayed pretty much to ourselves for the last two weeks, letting the kid get used to his new normal, which was anything but.

There was plenty for a boy to do on our island to keep his mind occupied, and most of it involved work. He jumped right in, tagging alongside Mr. Larry, doing anything his teacher asked of him.

He looked like a different person today. He kept his head up, eyes alert, and his complexion had filled in, skin darkening under the sub-tropical sun.

When he wasn't working with Larry, he was playing equally hard with Alberto and Tank.

Larry and I didn't want to rush him, but it was important for him to become social *and* get back to full-time schooling, so the lionfish safari was his first step toward Keys normal.

Larry and I had taken him and Alberto over to the north end of Content Passage every day for a week before making the trip down to the Anchor, and we'd killed and filleted several dozen of the invasive fish, adding a good eight pounds to the menu.

Upon arriving at the Rusty Anchor, Mason had been a little reserved due to all the people around, and he and Alberto had spent the morning down by the sea wall, throwing rocks into the water. Tank stayed close.

I was sitting at the bar, talking to Rusty and absently watching the news on the muted TV over the bar when my cell phone chirped. I looked at the screen. It was Stuart McCormick.

"Hey, Stu," I answered. "Are you still down island?"

"Ninety miles south of Nawlins, buddy," he replied. "Inspecting more rigs. Got a proposition for you, if you have a minute."

"Just waiting on some smoked lionfish," I replied. "What's up?"

"Your son mentioned you had a seaplane," he replied. "We just got a brand new submersible on board, and the test pilot and engineer are stuck in Key West. If you can help me get 'em up here where we are, I'll make sure you have first right of refusal on *Nomad,* and I'll personally instruct you."

"I can definitely do that," I said, sitting up. "How soon can they be ready?"

"Is tomorrow morning too early?" he asked.

"Text me the coordinates," I replied. "And tell them to meet me at the general aviation terminal at 0900."

"I appreciate it," Stu replied. "And I'll make you a sweet deal on *Nomad.*"

I ended the call just as the front door opened and Diane Pine came in, along with Kim and Marty.

"Was that *submarine* Stu?" Rusty asked. "What'd he want?"

I rose and gave my daughter a hug, then made room for them at the bar. Diane slid onto the stool next to Savannah as I grinned at Rusty. "He was just calling to sell me a sub."

Savvy turned to face me as the news came out of a commercial break. "Really? Which one?"

"*Nomad*," I told her. "The one with the robotic arms."

"Can you turn that up, Uncle Rusty?" Kim asked. "It's about to start."

"Sure thing," he replied, grabbing the remote. "What's about to start?" Then he turned to me. "Dibs on the first dive."

"The news story about Carver," Diane informed him, as Rusty turned up the volume.

"—over to Cassity Ortega, at the federal building," the anchorman said, as the screen shifted to a young female reporter standing with Diane and Sheena.

"I'm here now with Special Agent Sheena Chambers of the FBI," the reporter began, "along with Detective Sergeant Diane Pine of the Monroe County Sheriff's Office who broke the case. Detective Pine, can you tell us some background on what just happened in the federal courthouse this morning?"

"When was this?" Rusty asked, looking from Diane to the screen.

She was still wearing the same clothes.

"Based on a complaint from a minor child living in the Middle Keys," the on-screen Diane said, "I opened an investigation into one Dennis Carver of Miami for suspected sexual abuse of a child. The case moved forward quickly, and I contacted the Bureau's Miami field office and Agent Chambers."

"Thanks to Detective Pine's resourcefulness two weeks ago," Sheena said, "and the pile of digital evidence she gathered, we went to a federal judge for a warrant. Two weeks ago, we arrested Mr. Carver, even as more evidence of other heinous crimes was coming to light."

"So, what happened this morning?" the reporter reiterated.

Diane smiled at the camera. "When confronted with the suspect's own digital tracks, communications, and movements, and the possibility of a death sentence in one recently reopened murder investigation, Mr. Carver pled guilty."

"Guilty to what charges?" the reporter asked.

"Six counts of felonious kidnapping," Sheena replied, "six counts of sexual abuse of a minor child, six counts of cruelty to a child, and felony murder. More charges are pending."

The camera zoomed out so all three were in the frame as the reporter signed off. Sheena and Diane were both smiling like the proverbial Cheshire cat.

"Diane told me about your hunch, Dad," Kim said. "You were right; ballistics matched the slugs retrieved from Deuce's bulletproof glass to those that killed Sinclair and Mahoney."

"You did good," Savannah said, hugging Diane. "Both of you. We need more police like you."

"Thanks," Diane said, as Alberto, Mason, and Tank came in the back door. "But we couldn't have done it without Mason."

"Done what?" he asked, suddenly apprehensive that she was there.

Larry and Lauren followed them in, stopping short when they saw Diane.

"Dennis Carver was sentenced four hours ago," Diane said. "He'll serve life in a maximum-security federal prison, without any possibility of parole. It's over, Mason. He's gone for good."

The color literally flooded back into the boy's face as he exhaled.

"And I have more good news," I said. "All six of us are flying *Ocean Hopper* up north tomorrow to deliver two people to Stuart aboard *America*. We just bought *Nomad*."

The End

AFTERWORD

It took a while, but Rusty and Billy finally moved the submarine. It took a long time, because it would in real life. I no longer live in Florida, and haven't for almost twenty-five years, but having worked with environmental groups in my early years, I know the Sunshine State's wheels move very slowly.

But it's still not out of the woods.

As with many of my stories, the main plot for this one was pulled straight from the evening news. I have a list of plot ideas from news stories I've heard or read that's as long as your arm, and I try not to repeat a plot unless it's something that comes up in the news quite often.

Being the patriarch of three generations, aged two to forty-two, I hear about a lot of things involving them and their friends, and I wonder if I've shown them well enough, how to be resilient in the face of adversity, how to overcome whatever obstacles life throws in their paths, and how to stand up to injustice.

We are all bound by duty to seek justice for those who can't.

In case you're wondering, the submersible, *Nomad*, featured at the beginning and end of the story is a setup for my next book, *Cursed*, which will be out in the spring of 2026.

And since we had so much fun with some older characters returning, I decided to continue that with this book, with an impromptu "guys night" on the island. Also, since the main

AFTERWORD

antagonist, Manish Gupta, was still at large over these last few books, and unknown to Jesse and friends, I decided to bring him back, as well.

He's still out there.

My wife and I have had some struggles this past year, mostly physical. But by supporting each other, the way we always have, we've made it through another year. Having someone who you know will always be there for you makes life much better all the way around. I love you, G.

Thanks also to our kids, Nikki, Laura, Richard, and Jordan, our grandkids, Kira, Lexi, Jack, and Emily, and our great-grandson, Malakai, all of whom have supported my efforts for all these years and continue to do so. It's from them that I draw certain traits for my younger characters.

And of course, I owe Milli a belly rub and hearty "good girl" for her personality and all her many antics that I can see Tank doing, but at three times her size.

So, now you've met my cousin, Hoyt. He is the son of my mom's only brother, Willard "Chuck" Cooper, who was unknown to my uncle when he was born, and was adopted out at birth by his mother. Years ago, Hoyt found and reconnected with his birth mother, but not his biological father. He was a mystery.

Until I took the Ancestry DNA test. As with Rusty, Hoyt and I are a closer DNA match than first cousins ought to be, like my cousin, Debbie, whom I've known all my life, and who also took the test. Our fathers were brothers, but Hoyt and I had a higher DNA match.

There'd always been stories in our family about how my mother and Debbie's mother were distantly related. Now we know those stories must be true, even though we haven't yet found that connection.

AFTERWORD

Hoyt asked me to use his father's last name for this book, Cooper, instead of his real name, given him by his adoptive parents. Cooper is my mom's maiden name and my youngest daughter's middle name, so I was touched by his request.

My uncle didn't get married until late in his life, and he never had any children, though he'd always wanted a son. So, soon after they married, he and his wife adopted an infant boy and raised him as their own son. Uncle Chuck would have been over the moon to know that he had a biological son all those years and didn't know about him.

Of that, I'm certain.

My technical team gives me so much great feedback. Some are people I went to high school with, and old friends like that aren't afraid to hold back punches. Their input is "golden," as cousin Randy would say. He was also adopted, but by a different uncle. Some attributes of *Taranis* have yet to be revealed, mostly because the actual design isn't finished and mechanical details are still being tweaked by a couple of engineer friends. Who knows? Maybe one day, a boat like *Taranis* actually will be bult. I could just make those details up. After all, it is fiction, but I know some electrical or nautical engineer reading it would write me a blistering email if I was off by a kilowatt or two.

Some of *Taranis's* more intricate design features will be revealed in the next book, *Cursed*. But the tech people aren't ready to let us in on that just yet. A huge thanks to Deg Priest, Jason Hebert, Katy McKnight, Dana Vihlen, Mike Ramsey, Kim DeWitt, and Glenn Hibbert, for all your input.

While at the Novelists, Inc. (NINC) conference in September, I had dinner with my editor, Marsha Zinberg, and we tried to remember which was the first book she edited for me. As near as we could figure, she's edited the last thirty of my books, and early on, I had her re-edit the first two after I'd rewritten them. I have no formal education as a writer, only what I've learned from reading and Marsha's tutelage. She is truly a gem.

A big thanks to my final proofreader, Donna Rich, for always being available on short notice. By the time Marsha finishes and I do the first rewrite, it becomes difficult to schedule things, and Donna's never complained or taken more than a week to fix all the mistakes I made in rewrite.

And a special thanks to my audiobook narrator, good friend, and the always flexible Nick Sullivan. We try to schedule when he'll narrate, but the timing is often unknown until just before he's ready to go into the booth to record. Nick's not only narrated every word I've written in every book, but his performance still changes the way I write. Sometimes, I'll bring a character back just because I liked Nick's portrayal.

I owe my greatest gratitude to you, my readers. I know there are a few of you who read my first book, way back in 2013, and have been waiting for the next one ever since. Some of you may have read that first book a month or two ago, just finished the series, and have been waiting for this one. Whether you're new to my world (I'm not saying Wayne's World), or have been around since day one, the fact that y'all have now read thirty-four of my Jesse books humbles me to the core. Thank you.

Wayne

Made in United States
Orlando, FL
03 January 2026

Made in United States
Orlando, FL
03 January 2026